OTHER
CARNIVALS

NEW STORIES FROM BRAZIL

Published to celebrate the
first FlipSide, a festival of
Brazilian literature, music
and arts, in October 2013

OTHER CARNIVALS

NEW STORIES FROM BRAZIL

EDITED & TRANSLATED BY
ÁNGEL GURRÍA-QUINTANA

IMAGES BY
JEFFREY FISHER

FULL CIRCLE EDITIONS

Contents

Introduction
Ángel Gurría-Quintana

Brazilian songwriter Tom Jobim, one of the founders
of Bossa Nova, once advised an American photographer
against relocating to Rio de Janeiro. "Brazil", he said,
"is not for beginners."

Jobim's declaration was not only a light-hearted warning
about the dangers awaiting all gringos. It was also an
admonition against simplistic explanations and clichéd
depictions.

That was in the 1960s: the new musical style pioneered
by Jobim was taking off, and the country teetered towards
a military dictatorship. But what was true back then is even
more so half a century later, as Brazil basks in its BRIC status
and burnishes its credentials on the world stage.

Once lauded by Austrian novelist Stefan Zweig as a land of
the future (a dubious accolade), Brazil is very much the country
of the moment (equally dubious). But despite the swagger,
to most foreign observers it remains a place steeped in paradox:
a country whose perceived hedonism is in sharp contrast to its
deep-rooted conservatism; a country whose favelas are now
as iconic as its national monuments; a country that looms large
over the hemisphere, yet remains culturally isolated from its
Spanish-speaking neighbours; a country rippled by unrest even
as it lays claim to significant social and political achievements.

And notwithstanding the Order and Progress that have

propelled Brazil into the economic major leagues (just nudging its way ahead of the United Kingdom in the global rankings) some commonplaces refuse to die. Ask someone –anyone– what first comes to mind at the mention of Brazil, and the most likely answers will still be: beaches, football, carnival.

The twelve pieces of writing in this collection go some way to subverting those clichés. "We don't just listen to samba," says the aggrieved narrator of one of the stories. The protagonist of another explains why he has given up watching football. And while the piece of memoir that lends the volume its title evokes the world's most famous pre-Lenten celebration, it does so with oblique poignancy. *Carnaval* may seem inescapable, but there are always "other carnivals".

In Brazil, the expression is used more specifically to denote past times –as in, "I remember you from other carnivals", or even "Those were other carnivals" (meaning, "Those were the days"). There is indeed some looking back in these stories, but mostly they seem to be anchored in present-day Brazil, and offer illuminating snapshots of contemporary life.

Of course it is not the purpose of fiction to make us understand a place. The rationale underpinning this volume is not anthropological or documentary –although two of the texts are, in principle, works of non-fiction. These stories do not set out to explain anything, or even to ask pertinent questions, but simply to shine a light on certain nooks of human experience.

Which is not to say we cannot learn something from them. As Isaac Bashevis Singer was fond of reminding students, "the purpose of literature is to entertain and inform". So we are reminded, in the stories by Beatriz Bracher and Milton Hatoum, that Brazil is a nation of migrants. The entries by André Sant'Anna and Ferréz update us on the unstoppable expansion of evangelical churches. From Marcelino Freire's sketch-like piece, the closest here to social satire, we might glean some notions about Brazilian attitudes towards race.

João Anzanello Carrascoza's story of loss indicates that, despite (or perhaps because of) the gravitational pull of the country's urban centres, Brazil's rural hinterland occupies a significant place in writers' imaginations. Two contributions –one fictional (Andréa del Fuego) and the other journalistic (Reinaldo Moraes)—hint at the complex ways in which contemporary Brazilian authors engage with their foreign peers.

Adriana Lisboa and Cristovão Tezza show us that the greatest emotional revelations can occur at the quietest of moments. While Bernardo Carvalho's tale about a Brazilian trying to learn Mandarin brings us neatly back to the debate about emerging world powers.

As much as a variety of themes, this selection aspires to present a variety of styles. Some geographical considerations were at play –there is work by writers from the states of Amazonia, Minas Gerais, Pernambuco and Santa Catarina, though concentration on Rio de Janeiro and São Paulo was inevitable, and a reflection of national trends.

There is a wide generational spread, too. Some of the authors represented here were born when Rio de Janeiro was still the country's capital (Brasilia, the current capital, was established in 1960). Most of them experienced the military government and its shaky aftermath. Interestingly, the only story that tackles this dark period is by the youngest author in this group (Tatiana Salem Levy), born in Lisbon shortly before the end of the dictatorship.

None of these pieces demands any prior knowledge of Brazil, or its rich literary pedigree, for their enjoyment –though it helps to know that Tancredo Neves was the first Brazilian to win a direct presidential election after the fall of the military regime (he died on the eve of his inauguration), that Éder was an ill-tempered football player with the Brazilian national side in the 1980s, or that the actress Fernanda Montenegro is one of the country's national treasures. Beyond that, every text takes readers on its own unique course of discovery.

With a few notable exceptions, the scarcity of literature translated from Portuguese into English is a regular grievance. Familiarity with Brazilian fiction has not typically followed from Anglophone audiences' increasing familiarity with Brazilian music, design, film or architecture.

This may be changing. If there is, today, a heightened awareness of new Brazilian writing it is thanks to a handful of embattled publishers who have not lost faith in foreign authors and their English-language readers. It is also thanks to a cluster of dedicated translators (people like John Gledson, Margaret Jull-Costa or Alison Entrekin, to name only a few) who understand that their duty is to the reader as much as to the source material. *Granta* magazine's recent "Best of Young Brazilian Novelists" issue certainly amplified the buzz – one of the authors in that extraordinary line-up makes an appearance here, too.

Much of the credit for any mounting interest must lie with the Festa Literária Internacional de Parati (FLIP), which since 2003 has brought together Brazilian authors, publishers and journalists with their English-language colleagues (for a sense of what the experience is like, see Moraes' piece). It is no coincidence that the founders of FLIP are also the moving spirits behind this book.

Bossa Nova may have given way to many newer musical waves over the past five decades, but Tom Jobim's words still ring true. Brazil is not for beginners. And yet for anyone – beginners and veterans alike—seeking to open doors onto what a British newspaper recently called "the world's most exciting nation", there have never been so many points of entry. It is this anthology's aspiration to offer a dozen more.

A Burial and Other Carnivals
Milton Hatoum

I recalled carnivals past when I went to the burial of Dona
Faride, my friend Osman Nasser's mother. When I was
fourteen or fifteen years old, Osman was bordering on thirty
and was legendary in the placid Manaus of the sixties.

Placid? Not really. Of course the city was not yet that octopus
whose tentacles tear up the rainforest and reach across the
Rio Negro. But it was always a port for adventures, a place of
cyclical splendour and decadence, filled with fortune-hunters
from all corners of Brazil and beyond.

At the end of that sad afternoon –the weak sun filtered out
by dark and dense clouds—I recalled the carnival dances in
the clubs, and the street parties. The excitement began even
before carnival, on the afternoon when hundreds of people
welcomed Camélia at the Ponta Pelada airport, and the crowd
sang the carnival march Oh gardener, Why are you so sad,
What happened to you? and then the throng escorted the
gigantic doll all the way to the Olympico club. I don't know
if it was legal to use the inhalers known as lança perfume,
but those glass vials certainly refreshed our carnival nights,
the ether mixing with the sweat coming off bodies and with
the early morning dew.

We did not watch Rio de Janeiro's samba schools on parade;
in fact, there were no televisions in Manaus: carnival meant
four sleep-deprived days and their sleepless nights, moving

from the city's squares to its clubs. Fat Monday, at the Rio Negro Athletic Club, was the climax of the carnival revelry that ended at the Adolpho Lisboa Municipal Market, where we saw or thought we saw costumed oversized fish and masked fishmongers. There were also mermaids, hoarse from all the singing, semi-nude and tousle-haired odalisques, dethroned princesses, carnival celebrants dressed in rags, paupers who were given a bowl with banana porridge or fried jaraqui fish. The drunkest revellers dived into the river to soothe their hangovers, others argued with vultures on the beach or tried to find the girlfriends they had lost at some point of the merrymaking, when no one belonged to anyone and carnival was a hallucinatory miracle. How many men cried on the beach, their faces full of confetti and their hearts wrung dry.

"Great is God our Lord", sing relatives and friends at the burial, while I recall that yuletide night when Dona Faride handed out gifts to guests and party-crashers who wanted to celebrate Christmas eve with the Nassers.

There is the tree covered by colourful parcels; in the living room, the table is laden with finger food, patio lights shine on the fountain encircled by children; old Nasser, sitting in the rocking chair, smokes a cigar with the pose of a perfect patriarch. I hear the voice of Oum Kalsoum on the 78 rpm record, I hear happy cries, I see Osman's nine sisters dancing for their father; then they offer him dates and pistachios that have travelled from the far side of the world to that small and diffuse Orient in the centre of Manaus.

Now the women sing praises to God, recite the Lord's Prayer, and I look away towards the stilled mango trees that cast afternoon shade on the ground, centenarian mango trees, among the few remaining in the city. It seems that only the dead have the right to shade, Manaus' living toil under the sun. I glance at the top of the mausoleum and see a star and a crescent moon made of metal –or is it stone?–, the symbols of Islam, old Nasser's religion. It is one of the Muslim mausoleums in the São João Batista cemetery, although the mother that is descending into the earth was a Catholic.

I recognise friends' faces, revellers from times past, and there, between two tombs, kneeling and bowing low, I see the fruit seller who, in my youth, carried the yields of an entire orchard on his head. The singing stops in the calm of dusk, and life, when evoked far into the past, seems like a dream. I embrace my orphan friend, who whispers an Arab proverb into my ear: A mother is worth a world.

Soon it will be carnival...

The Language of the Future
Bernardo Carvalho

It all begins when the student of Chinese decides to learn Chinese. And that happens precisely when he starts thinking that his own language cannot express what he wants to say. That also means, of course (and therein lies the contradiction), that the possibility of saying what he wants to say is not contained in the Chinese language itself, but in a language he can only imagine, because it is so difficult to learn. It is in that language that he would like to tell his story. Let's call that language Chinese, for want of a better name. He would like to say, in Chinese: "It is a cliché that travelling helps you escape heartbreak, but you can never escape a cliché," but he can't, because he never got as far as that lesson. The student of Chinese is on his way to China to escape from the past seven years of married life, six of them spent studying Chinese, when he notices at the check-in queue the Chinese teacher who disappeared two years earlier, abandoning suddenly and with no explanation the private tuition she gave him at the school of Chinese, forcing the student to continue his course with a substitute. Since the teacher's disappearance, the student of Chinese had harboured an urgent need to find out her story, and her unexpected reappearance at the check-in queue seems like the perfect opportunity.

The first time he saw her, he thought she was not Chinese. It is true that the student of Chinese had been irritated by the discovery that his old teacher had been replaced without anyone consulting him. It was not the first time. No teacher stayed for long at the school. She was the third one he had met in three years. The first was fired because she had needed to travel back to China with her mother. Since the school offered no holidays or leave, no one could ever stop teaching Chinese, ever. That first teacher's trip to China, accompanying her old mother to see a brother who was on his deathbed, was considered abandonment of employment, and was accordingly punished with just dismissal (to keep up appearances, since she didn't even have a contract).

Her replacement allowed herself to be exploited while it was convenient. Some months later, after collecting in a little notebook the phone numbers of all the school's students she had taught, she asked to be paid more, gaining an upper hand on the head teacher, who would normally have been exploiting and hoodwinking the employees.

The third Chinese teacher welcomed him at the school gate, with a Chinese smile (and the adjective implies no form of prejudice, as the student of Chinese insists every time he is accused of being a racist; yes, it is merely an approximate translation of an untranslatable expression), singing in Chinese, to dispel any doubts that she was the new teacher. From the beginning, every time a teacher was replaced, the student of Chinese had felt hard done by, unable to understand the reasons for the replacement and unable to do anything about them, no matter how accustomed he had become to the previous teacher's methods (and no matter how bad those methods were), since he was only told about the changes (if at all) once they had happened, when there was no going back. To make matters worse, the new teacher, singing at the school gate, did not seem Chinese –and not only physically, even though she had the same indecipherable smile. She spoke a language that was even more incomprehensible than that of previous teachers. Her Chinese did not even relate to pinyin transliteration, the phonetic transcription in the Latin alphabet that should in theory allow westerners to reproduce the sounds of characters, or at least imagine what they sound like. Besides the cartoonish confusion of "r" and "l" that generally afflicts the Chinese, she also replaced the sound of "sh" with "s" and vice-versa, saying "shun" when the sun was out or trying to explain to the bemused student how it was "sining" brightly in the sky.

What happens at the airport is very strange indeed. When the student of Chinese enters the departures hall, the teacher he hasn't seen in two years is already at the check-in queue, holding hands with a girl of around five, Chinese like her. Everything is Chinese. The plane is going to China. The girl does not let go of the teacher's hand. The student of Chinese, who could never understand what might have caused the teacher to leave half way through lesson 22 of the fourth book in the intermediate course, is surprised to see her holding a little girl's hand at the check-in queue of the same flight that will, in theory, take him to Shanghai. As far as he knew, when she was still teaching him two years ago, the teacher had no children. She is a young woman of twenty-seven, slender and fragile, with skeletal arms and mousy brown hair, thinning, limp and with split ends, as if straightened with a hot iron. The hair colour is, for him, an anomaly, as is the Chinese teacher's skin, the same colour as her hair. If her hair had not always been that colour, since the day she welcomed him singing at the school gate, he would have thought it was tinted. The student of Chinese approaches her and calls out her name. The teacher turns around, scared, as if she'd seen a ghost. She is paler than she was when she taught him. She starts to tremble. She doesn't know how to react or what to say, fumbles the plane tickets and passports she clutches in the hand with which she is also pushing the luggage trolley, since the other is holding the girl's hand. She drops the passports and tickets, but when the student is going to pick them up she lets go of the child's hand and lunges for them. The girl starts crying. He says, in his own language, since the Chinese he learned in six years is not even good enough to make small talk to his teacher at the check-in queue: "What a coincidence! You left our course half way through. You disappeared. I was worried. I even called your mobile phone, to find out if anything had happened to you." But before she can answer, once again holding passports, tickets and the girl, a man pushes the student of Chinese from behind, shoving him to one side

and interrupting the conversation, and grabs the teacher by the arm. She barely has time to react or cry, as well she might. She wants to plead for the girl, but before she is even able to say "no", or pass out (and there would be good reasons for that), the man who is grabbing her by the arm says into her ear: "Stay calm. Don't say a word. Now, you're coming with me. They'll take care of the bags." She looks at the luggage in the trolley like someone watching the future go down the drain. The man follows her gaze and asks, as if on the brink of indignation: "You didn't put it in the bags, did you?" She shakes her head to say no. She sways her head, with her eyes open wide. The man takes the girl in his arms and pushes the

Chinese teacher out of the queue. The girl, who had stopped crying momentarily when the stranger intervened, cries again. He drags the teacher across the concourse. Before she disappears from view, leaving the student of Chinese behind, next to the abandoned luggage trolley, the teacher turns to him and says something in Chinese that he does not understand. The Chinese passengers who are standing in the queue, and who might have understood something, don't dare look at her or at him, as if looking were enough to end up like that Chinese teacher. Beyond simply paying no attention to the student of Chinese, they pretend they haven't seen anything. In China, no one needs to go to school to learn how to behave.

A few seconds later, another man appears behind the student of Chinese and asks: "Where did they go?"
The student doesn't know what to reply. The man continues without waiting for an answer: "Are the bags yours? Are they hers? Do you know her, were you with her? You're coming with me." The student of Chinese, who has heard that phrase used before, says in his own language: "I can't. I don't want to miss my flight." The man insists. "You're coming with me. I'm a police officer," and flashes his badge. The student of Chinese hesitates for a few seconds before following him, worried and apprehensive, while the policeman pushes the trolley with the teacher's luggage into an elevator. They walk to a windowless office in the police's upper floor offices. Once inside, the policeman closes the door and begins the interrogation. He wants to know what the Chinese woman said to him, from across the departures hall, in Chinese, while his fellow police officer dragged her away. The student of Chinese now says in his own language:

"Why? What do you mean why? Because I studied Chinese. I didn't study English or Spanish. Chinese is the devil's language. So it's normal that I can't understand anything even after studying for six years. It's normal. Even German, by comparison, is a piece of cake. Obviously I couldn't speak to her. How do you expect me to know what she said? In Mandarin, the same syllable has four different meanings. You didn't know that? Four. And there are some other languages that have even more tones. Cantonese, for instance, which is another form of Chinese. It's like shooting blindfolded. You hit the target if you're lucky. You're a policeman, you know what I mean. Four tones. Not to mention homophones. What are homophones? What do you mean, what are homophones? Homo means the same. As in homosexual. Phono means sound. The same sound. And you expected me to understand? How did I meet her? Like I said, at the school of Chinese. Sorry, but what language are we speaking here? It's just that you appear not to understand me. At the school of Chinese. AT-THE-SCHOOL-OF-CHI-NESE! I'm going to miss my flight if we carry on like this. You tell me what you need to know and I'll reply, okay? What? No, sorry, sorry, I'll calm down, it's just that I'm going to miss my flight. No, of course, I know, I know, you're in charge, you're in charge. I'll catch my flight if you want me to. I'll say it again: you're in charge here. That's right, I'll forget about the flight. Ready, I've forgotten about the flight. From the beginning, sure, let's start from the beginning. I met her at the school of Chinese. That's it. Why did I study Chinese? It's the language of the future. It just is. One day, the whole world will understand and speak only Chinese.

Even us, this interrogation, will have to be carried out in Chinese. Whoever doesn't speak it will be fucked. Have you thought about that? I don't want to be fucked. No one wants to. Of course, of course. No swearing here. You're the boss. Okay, it's not an interrogation. You don't have to shout. We're having a conversation. So, I went to learn Chinese. There will be a lot of business in the future for anyone who speaks Chinese. Foreign trade, import-export. You know that in ten years' time, according to economists' forecasts, the 'scenario' [*using his hands to do air-quotes*] –isn't that what they call it? – the 'scenario' will be China becoming the world's largest economy. And when they invade Brazil, I want to welcome them in Chinese, singing. Want to know how you say it? You don't want to know? That was how she welcomed me on her first day of lessons, at the school gate, singing a welcome in Chinese, *huang ying, huang ying*, as if I were one of those little Chinese kids on the first day of nursery school, and I couldn't understand a thing. She sang and sang, smiling, *huan ying, huan ying*, and I, pretending I knew, repeated the first syllable, *huan huan*, which was the only part I'd caught, not knowing what I was saying, but syllable is just a figure of speech, because in Chinese there are no words with more than one syllable, in fact they don't have syllables, and there I was dancing with her at the school gate, though dancing is also just a figure of speech, swaying from side to side, with loose arms, and smiling at her, echoing that first syllable, *huan huan*. The tone was wrong, of course. Do you know that hearing aids don't work in China? That's right...I read about it the other day. You know why? Because Chinese is a tonal language. That's right! And tones aren't words; they're more like music. That fucks things up. The hearing aid can't tell the difference.

Of course, sorry for swearing. No swearing here, not even in Chinese. No, no, I'm not trying to be funny, no, honestly, sorry, I just don't want to miss my flight. It leaves now, at six. Right, I've forgotten all about it. Drugs? What do you mean?
No, I didn't take any drugs. I didn't take any sedatives, either. This is how I am. I get nervous when I'm travelling. I'm calmer now. I'm calmer. Don't worry. From the start. Yes. So, she welcomed me singing *huan ying, huan ying.* The song is longer: *gao xing wo jian dao ni.* No? Okay, you don't want to hear, that's fine. I had to learn it by heart, didn't I? If not I wouldn't pass. A school for grownups, yes, of course it was a school for grownups. But their methods were for children, weren't they? That's how they teach reading and writing in China, so why should it be different here, with grownups? If those little Chinese kids learn like that, why shouldn't we? I don't know, I didn't invent that method, but I believe that's what they do, you can ask them yourself when they invade us. Though who knows what will happen to anyone who doesn't speak Chinese when they invade. But we're friends, if you're in trouble just tell them you know me. Right, right, sorry, of course, the Chinese teacher. I'll tell you what I know. I could never figure out where she got her clothes. She was very creative. You know, like fashion designers? She made things out of fabric. She must have bought it down on Rua 25 de Março, because she had no money for clothes, but she was always wearing something new. So she had to be creative. She added Chinese touches to some cheap fabric. If you saw her on the street, you'd never imagine she didn't have a cent to her name. Because she really didn't. In one of our first classes, she asked me a question and her eyes gleamed when I gave her an answer, which I forget now, in fact I forget what her question was, but she said she too couldn't

stand people being nosy about her life, with gleaming eyes,
as if she had finally found a fellow traveller, she said Chinese
people have no shame –and they really don't, no sooner have
you met one than they want to know if you're married.
She seemed happy to know that I didn't want to know anything
about her life. And she didn't ask any more about mine.
No more than the occasional question every now and then,
of course. Like my Chinese horoscope sign. We had a whole
class about the Chinese horoscope. So she had to ask, didn't
she? She's clever. When she wanted to find something out,
she'd find a way. She would say an animal's name, in Chinese,
of course, it wouldn't have been a Chinese class otherwise,
and I had to make up a sentence. For instance: the rat is
resilient, the horse is strong, the tiger is fierce, and so on.
And then, at the end, she asked what my sign was in the
Chinese horoscope. And I said: Rat. And she: Me too!
And then, since we had more in common than I expected,
even if she was Chinese, I asked if she had also been born in
1960. She pulled a completely Chinese face. I understood a few
things about the language and the culture, because I'd been
studying them for three years. So I apologised: Oh, sorry, you
were born in 1972. You know that the Chinese horoscope has
a twelve-year cycle, don't you? So, since she still had that
expression on her face, I had to apologise again, because she
was born in '84. I was wrong about her age by twenty-four
years. Look, I'm no good with faces. I don't know how I can
help. Can I go now? Look, my flight leaves in...Of course,
no, you're right. Yes, I understand, the flight doesn't matter,
I'll go to China when you say. Of course. I forgot to say that,
before her, I had some other Chinese teachers, always at the
same school, and, one after the other, they always disappeared

without any explanation. I would arrive at my classes in the morning and find a new teacher. It was like that the day she welcomed me, singing *huan ying, huan ying*. No, I won't sing again, don't worry. It was just for you to understand.

Because, if not, it doesn't add up, does it? I want to avoid any misunderstandings. I couldn't carry on with what I was saying if I didn't explain that I'd had other teachers before her and that I knew the pronunciation from the north, which is how the other teachers spoke, the ones who disappeared without an explanation, because for me it was a shock when she started speaking with her southern accent. Yes, from the south. She's from the south. That's right. In Chinese, or rather, in the transliteration system they invented so we could understand how to pronounce their characters, many words start with ch, which sounds like tch, or with sh and zh, which sound as if they were a j, and others that start with c, pronounced like ts; with an s, which sounds just like our s, and with z, which sounds as if it were tz. You don't want to know? It's easy, just...Right. Okay. But in the south of China they mix everything up. So she would say shea sore. And I'd say: it's not shea, it's sea; it's not sore, it's shore. And she'd ask: What did I just say? Shea, sore. It could drive you crazy. In Portuguese, that's not such a problem. But in Chinese, a language of monosyllables, *cha, sa, cho, so, zu, zhu, cu, ku, dong*... no, I'm not swearing, it's just that if I could hardly understand my teachers from the north, even less the southern one. And that was driving me nuts at the start. Whatever had happened to my previous teacher, with the Pekinese accent? I have to digress here, just so you can understand, and I don't want to sound racist –for the love of God!—but a friend of mine, Jewish in fact, so he can't be anti-Semite (which proves that I'm not either, doesn't it, because

I'm his friend), said to me the other day that the Chinese were
Asia's Jews. And, you know what, I agree. Didn't you ask for my
opinion? It's just that if I don't explain you won't understand
my story. Very well, whatever you say. Me? No, not a racist.
Whoever heard of a racist Brazilian? What I meant was that
the Chinese have no respect for human beings. Even less
for employees. The Chinese were born to exploit others.
It couldn't be otherwise. Life in China is worth nothing.
Just look at how many people are executed every year,
over nothing! There are so many of them. And they are a
money-oriented people. And this isn't just my opinion,
no. Everyone knows. Very well, I'll be quiet. Okay, okay, I won't
say a thing. You don't have to shout. All that just to say that the
school's owner paid the teachers so badly that none of them
stayed. When they asked for a raise, they were sent away,
kicked out. And the supply of teachers dwindled to the point
that they had to hire a teacher from the south, who called the
sea-shore a shea-sore. But I grew fond of her, you know, and
not only because deep down she was a good teacher (even if the
little I speak today is all wrong, I learned more with her than
with any of the other teachers with their Pekinese accents).
Because she did not like prying people, she started telling me
about her life without my having asked. All in small doses,
obviously. But the moment I seemed interested, and wanted to
know more and asked her a personal question, she would
interrupt what she was saying and get back to the lesson.
And there was no point in insisting, she smiled and changed
the subject and only took it up again weeks later, whenever she
felt like it again and when I least expected it. It was a very sad
story. All Chinese stories are very sad. It couldn't have been
any other way. Can you imagine being born in southern China?

You can't? You can't imagine anything? Well try to imagine being born in a village in southern China, after the application of the One Child Policy. You don't know what that is? China has more than 1.3 billion people. Imagine if they didn't have a birth control policy! The Chinese want to have children. Everyone wants children, but the Chinese want male children. And when she was born, her mother already had two girls. She was already beyond what the law allowed. But she wasn't going to stop until she had a boy. If people's lives are worthless in China, a woman's is worth even less. There are too many. When her mother became pregnant for the third time, she hid in another village where nobody knew her. She almost died during childbirth. She had the child on her own. But, instead of a boy, she gave birth to my Chinese teacher! She did not know what to do with that waste of a child. Another girl! And, in order not to dump her in a rubbish heap, which is what we do here, she left the newborn outside her neighbour's door. It made no difference to the neighbour, who already had seven children, all of them hungry and working themselves to death out in the fields the whole day. And she was even poorer than my Chinese teacher's birth mother. But she was a woman with a big heart in that village somewhere near the world's arse. Sorry. My mistake. No, I completely forgot, of course. It's just that arse isn't a rude word for me. She only discovered she was the neighbour's daughter when her schoolmates began making fun of her face, which was just as scruffy as the neighbour's. The birth mother emigrated to Canada, with her husband and daughters, and it was only once my teacher was here, and teaching me Chinese, that she called her mother, in Canada, and they both cried a lot on the phone, until her mother remembered it was a collect call and said it was going to be

expensive and hung up. I think they spoke once again.
The only thing her birth mother wanted to know was why my
teacher hadn't found a husband. And she didn't like anyone
asking about her life. It was she who told me that she worked
in a church. And that she was married to Jesus. I didn't ask
anything. She talked about her life in no particular order,
just random fragments, out of the blue, and so I never knew
how she arrived here, because she disappeared before telling
me. If I asked, she would change the subject and get back to the
class. She was a missionary at the church. She went from house
to house, knocking on the doors of other miserable Chinese
like her, down on Rua 25 de Março, with the Bible in one hand,
to take them to church, like someone had once taken her in
China. She said she started here, that she wasn't in any church
before, had never heard of one, but who knows, because
churches are banned in China, and she wasn't going to expose
her missionary colleagues' clandestine work in China by
saying that she had been lobotomised by them over there, was
she? If you want to know, I think she entered the church in
China. One day when she failed to show up, because she was ill,
and she was often ill because she was quite frail, the head
teacher taught me lots of rude words in Chinese (no, I won't
say any, don't worry, and you wouldn't understand them
anyway), but asked me not to tell my teacher at our next lesson
because she could be offended. And perhaps you'll agree that
it's unlikely that a twenty-something year old girl could not
tolerate swearing in Chinese, especially if she is Chinese
herself, and was born speaking the devil's language, unless
she's a member of a church. She gave me one of her church's
magazines: 'Satan is the invisible master of the universe'.
One day, when I entered the classroom, she was crying.

She wanted to know if her classes were bad, if I considered her a bad teacher. No, no! Why? She'd found out that no other teacher at the school was paid as poorly as she was.

She brought up the question of a raise with the school's owner, a money-grabbing Chinese like all others, and there's no racial prejudice in that, for the love of God, it's in the newspapers, just read the news, and she told my teacher that she got paid what she deserved and that no other student wanted to be taught by her. Only me. I tried to explain politely that it might be her use of s and sh, but that it hardly mattered, because she was an excellent teacher. She thanked me. She even said that, were it not for me, she would have left and returned to China. That's why I can't understand why she abandoned me half way through lesson 22 of the fourth book in the intermediate course. And now, when she reappears and has a chance to explain, your colleague takes her away. Where did you take my Chinese teacher? What? Drugs? What drugs? She's a Christian. What language are we speaking here, anyway?"

Lost Time
Tatiana Salem Levy

Lúcia makes sure her husband has driven off before going to the maid's room and rummaging in the wardrobe for the suitcase with André's photographs and letters.

She asked for the day off from work a week ago, right after the unexpected phone call. She was on her way out, the front door already open, when she heard the insistent ringing. At the other end of the line, a vaguely familiar yet unrecognisable voice asked for her. Then it announced:

—We've decided to bury André.

Bury André? The statement echoed in Lúcia's head like the lingering sound of waves after an afternoon by the seaside. A single phrase, and time was wiped away, as if the almost forty years separating André's death from that morning, when she was simply on her way to work, were an empty space. A vaccum between past and present, now joined in the firmly intoned phrase. Lúcia is no longer twenty years old, and almost nothing in her life, or in her body, reminds her of the young woman she once was. Only that phrase could bring back what she kept hidden for so long.

—But... Did you find the body?

The burial was scheduled for noon. Years had passed before André's family was offered any compensation by the courts. The lack of a body, or of any photographs or documents, had made the process more difficult: there was no certain proof, other than his relatives' certainty. Whatever proof existed remained hidden in archives, under lock and key. Despite the obstacles, he was finally registered as disappeared. The Brazilian state assumed its responsibility, and André's family then decided to have a burial without a body.

The suitcase is made of hard leather, old and dusty. The last time Lúcia saw its contents was twenty years ago, when she, her husband and her son moved to the apartment in Jardim Botanico, where they live to this day. Inside the suitcase is a blue box with white polka dots, a gift from André. The faded photographs within show a slender Lúcia, different from today's Lúcia, and a vigorous and handsome André. Beneath the photographs, the letters she received from him, the billets-doux, the words of love scrawled on scraps of paper. She turns everything over, hurls photos and letters on the floor, anxious to find something: an amulet shaped like an eye that André had worn around his neck since the day his grandmother gave it to him for his birthday. The amulet Lúcia was carrying on that momentous day when fate, out of mockery, decided to invert their roles just once. And forever.

*

Lúcia and André met while they were still at school, at Pedro II, in the city centre. They were both fifteen and together they discovered love and politics. Lúcia was a politicised teenager; from an early age, when she heard her parents grumble about the coup, despondent, she decided to contribute to her country's future. At first she became involved in school politics until, persuaded by a friend, she joined the Communist Party. She brought André with her and, though to begin with he was no more than a young man in love, he soon proved to be as engaged with political issues as she was. When the Party was banned, they joined the Alliance for National Liberation, ready to take up weapons against the dictatorship.

Weapons? They sometimes wondered: is this the best way forward? And if we're defeated? And if we die? And if? The questions crossed their minds, especially in those rare moments when they were alone, in bed, or sharing a long bath. But time was pressing and, although fear seemed determined to stay with them, they were forced to ignore it.

*

Lúcia and André have just arrived at a two-storey house, in Jacarepaguá, where they have to stay for an indefinite period of time. The house is relatively large, but simple and somewhat run down. The white paint is flaking off the walls, and there is hardly any furniture. They don't care in the least. Only two things matter to them: revolution and love, in no particular order.

They have been in that struggle for over three years. They have lost great companions, and the net is closing in. They are both wanted by the police, street posters and newspaper notices show their faces. They know they can die, but they refuse to leave the country, there is still hope. The house is, in a certain way, a new start.

*

In the shower, Lúcia remembers details of every moment they lived together. She thinks of the close embraces she welcomed with such happiness, but also with some apprehension: Would they embrace the following morning? So young, such eagerness, such willingness to fight, and already scared of dying. Little by little they began losing dear friends, hasty tears squeezed between a speech and an assault. Little by little, certainties gave way to doubts, but it was necessary to go on fighting.

Lúcia's code name was Vera; André's was Carlos. They only called each other by their real names in private. Now, as warm water washes over her body, she hears André whispering in her ear. And laughs. She laughs and cries at the same time. Sometimes she wishes life had turned out differently. Guilt always pains those who stay behind.

*

They spend the weekend doing nothing, the whole house to themselves, as it has been for the past month. Outside, a storm started not long ago. André goes up the stairs to find Lúcia, who is resting in the bedroom. He stands in front of the window and gazes at the rain, listening to the sound of water drops falling on the ground in the back yard. The blue-grey sky will soon blacken as night falls.

—Come here, lie down.

André remains silent, his thoughts distant. Lúcia insists.

—Come here, come.

André turns to her, with a sweet smile.

—Yes, comrade, your wish is my command.

—Silly!

—Shall I turn off the light?

—No, leave it on.

—Brazil's most feared revolutionary is scared of the dark?

—I'm not scared of the dark...

—Then why leave the light on?

*

From the bed, the eye-shaped amulet observes Lúcia getting dressed. She takes a black dress out of her wardrobe, a gift from Roberto, her husband. She is suddenly shocked by her own act. Confusion, indecision: attend André's funeral wearing another man's gift? The amulet watches her searchingly, and she feels she has in some way betrayed a man to whom she had promised so much.

The black dress makes time expand again. Yes, she had a life. Between André's death and his burial, she did many things. She went into exile in Mexico for almost ten years. It was there that she studied economics and got married for the first time, to Gabriel, father of her only son, who ended up being raised by Roberto. She travelled around Central America, went to Cuba countless times. She kept on fighting as long as she remained in Mexico, and only gave up after returning to Brazil, as if she could no longer do it here. She worked in business, taught, began a life that she would have repudiated before, but which had since become convenient. She was no longer worried about great changes, but about small moments of happiness.

Lúcia feels the weight of time: the time in which she did so much, the time in which she did nothing. She never forgot André, her most intimate secret, a story she never told anyone and that only the amulet knows. The amulet that watches her now as intently as it did forty years ago. She wishes that things had happened differently, that events were not irreparable.
—I should have died, not him.

With her hair tied in a bun, light make up around her eyes, a dab of blush, Lúcia transfers her possessions from one handbag to another. It's the banal gestures that scare her:
–I'm alive. She is already on her way out when she remembers the amulet. She returns to pick it up and twists her mouth into

an ironic smile. The eye in the bag, the black dress, and Lúcia is ready to go. When she closes the door behind her she realises that she is, indeed, André's widow.

*

—We've been here for three months. Should we give up?
—Give up?
—Yes...Sometimes I think we're just wasting time.
—Would you rather believe that nothing is happening? That the dictatorship doesn't exist?
—No.
—So?
—It's just that sometimes I'm afraid.
—Me too.
—Really afraid. Afraid of being caught, afraid of torture, afraid of dying.
—I'm afraid of losing you.
—So am I.
—If I get caught, will you wait for me?
—If you get caught, I'll get caught with you.
—Will you wait for me?
—I'll wait. You?
—Me too.
—Promise?
—Promise.

*

It is drizzling softly when Lúcia arrives at Caju cemetery. There are more people than she expected, all gathered in the chapel, around the coffin. She seeks out a familiar face, but cannot identify anyone. In the end, it is not their features but their tears that make her recognise the sisters. Mônica, the elder, bears the evidence of her age in her plastic surgery. The pulled-back cheeks, the overstretched eyes, are proof that she is trying to deny she is already a grandmother. Renata, the younger sister who was once so close to André and is today mother to two teenagers, holds Lúcia tight in her arms and breaks down in sobs, unashamed. Her former sister-in-law's body does not correspond to her memory of it. When they first met, Renata was a child who dragged her teddy bear around the apartment and adored Lúcia, who always found a way to take her out for ice cream, or a film and some popcorn. For years, Renata thought about those moments. For years she remembered the last time they saw each other, Lúcia's kind words, while André hurried to pack their rucksack: —We're going travelling, darling. But we'll be back, I promise!

It took her a while, but the years taught Renata that promises made in times of war are not to be kept, even though the hope of seeing her brother again was always there. A hope that not even unfeasibility can destroy. In the younger sister's embrace, Lúcia feels the desperate longing for André's embrace.

Rui, the father, so wizened, his back curved, is sitting right behind the daughters and the grandchildren. When she pats his bald head and asks: —Do you remember me?, Lúcia understands that a father suffers as much as a mother when his child dies. But his voice is gentle, he must have forgotten that he used to rebuke his daughter-in-law, convinced that she was responsible for André's political engagement.

Lúcia doesn't know most of the people who are there, they must be friends of the sisters, she supposes. Almost all her comrades-in-arms died, almost all were registered as disappeared by the state. Few survived from her group.

But survivors from other groups are there, friends of André. Lúcia joins their circle. She has remained in touch with some of them all along, even if sporadically; others, she hasn't seen since the early seventies. Surrounded by them, she feels a trace of happiness, the comfort of those who have stayed behind. Without paying too much attention, she listens to those stories from the past that they are so fond of remembering, and which give the funeral a more lighthearted air.

Lúcia approaches Mônica and Renata carrying the amulet she has just taken out of her bag in the palm of her hand.

—Can I put it in there?

—In there?

—Yes...

The sisters can't hide their surprise: She wants to open the coffin? They glance at each other, amazed, don't know what to say. Silence reigns over the following few seconds, which pass much slower than seconds usually do.

—I understand, it's just that...

—You don't need to explain, says Mônica, so brusque and assertive that Renata cannot question her.

Lúcia thanks them with a simple smile, bowing her head. She walks unhurriedly towards the coffin. The atmosphere in the chapel now feels lighter. The sisters are no longer crying, and there is such a buzz that it could almost be said, were it not for the context, that people are having a good time. The lid is heavy, Lúcia struggles to open it. Some people wonder what she's trying to do. Some people think of helping her, but no one moves. Finally she manages to open a narrow slit and put her arm into the coffin. The amulet slides through her fingers and falls. The noise echoes through the room and everyone turns to see her. Lúcia hurriedly pulls out her arm. The clang of the lid shutting on the coffin is less frightening than the noise made by the amulet.

But she is forgiven. And relieved. She has just buried her greatest secret, her greatest guilt.

*

André and Lúcia are in bed, late at night. That afternoon, they were supposed to meet with a comrade who did not show up at the rendezvous.

—We'll have to leave this place.

—Calm down, there was no one there, we're safe.

—Security rule number one: we'll have to move house.

—Tomorrow.

—Today, now.

—Calm down, we'll leave tomorrow. No one knows we're here.

—Okay, tomorrow. But no later.

They are both calmer now, they breathe with relief, despite the ongoing tension. The will awake before sunrise and get on the road. They don't know where, the only thing that matters is leaving the house. They know that, in some way, they were happy there, although the shortness of time doesn't allow them to dwell on it. They need to rest, the road ahead could be long.

—I'm thirsty.

—Me too.

—Heads or tails?

—Heads.

—Tails.

André is getting out of bed when Lúcia says:

—It's okay, I'll go.

André smiles. He is so tired he doesn't argue. He merely takes an amulet in the shape of an eye that is hanging around his neck, his lucky charm, a present from his grandmother that he's worn since she gave it to him. He hands it over to Lúcia.

—Here. To protect you.

—On my way to the kitchen?

—You never know. There might be a big bad wolf lurking on the way.

Lúcia laughs. So does André. They kiss, and Lúcia goes downstairs. In the kitchen, she fills two glasses with water, takes a sip and, before closing the fridge, nibbles on some cheese that will stay behind after they have left. She hears a strange sound, far away, and freezes. Is she hearing things?
No, she is not hearing things. The sound of footsteps approaching is as real as the two glasses in front of her.
She grabs them quickly, in a flash of clear-mindedness, and hides in the gap between the fridge and the kitchen door, the one leading out to the back yard, her heart racing, almost in her throat. The front door comes crashing down, she can feel in her feet the floor trembling beneath the men who have just rushed in. They shout, spread out around the house, they briefly look around the ground floor, the living room, the kitchen, the toilet. "Up there, quickly", says one of them. Lúcia's hands tremble as she opens the door to the back yard as delicately as possible, noiselessly. She is walking across the yard, bent over, when she hears André's shouts mixing with the policemen's. She automatically starts running and jumps over the low fence into the neighbouring house, which is empty. The owners left carrying luggage two weeks ago and haven't returned. She looks around, doesn't know where to go, doesn't know whether to flee, to stop, to return.

Finally she notices a shed behind the house, where gardening utensils are kept. Luckily for her, the door is open. In fact the door doesn't close, and Lúcia finds a place among hoes, shears, pitchforks, spades and sacks full of soil, in near darkness, except for the sky's weak light. Her body trembles from head to toes, her heart not slowing down for even an instant. She knows they will find her sooner or later, it's a matter of time.

But time goes by, and they don't appear. Lúcia sees the dawn through the crack in the door. She is still standing when the sun reaches the shed's entrance, and only then does she allow herself what fear had prevented her from doing, she clutches the amulet in her hands and cries, no longer worried that someone will hear her high-pitched sobs.

*

The rain is still falling, persistent, after the funeral. Lúcia drives back home. Some images come back into her head: the lovely memorial speech by friends; the Vandré song that almost everyone sang along to; Renata's sweet words about her brother. The funeral was more of a meeting than a farewell.

It is two o'clock in the afternoon and there is little traffic. Lúcia feels like stepping on the accelerator and driving on, with no obstacles. The smile on her face is so conspicuous that drivers in other cars who stop alongside her at the traffic lights smile too. Lúcia feels renewed, ready to start over, like the day she arrived at that white house in Jacarepaguá, with André. She turns on the radio and recognises the tune, her son listened to it all the time, repeatedly, in the late eighties. She feels like getting up and dancing. She knows she no longer has the time that passed, but she still has all the time in the world.

The Cut
Cristovão Tezza

"If only he'd get a haircut," the geography teacher heard
someone whisper as the class ended, and was as startled as
if someone had made a direct accusation. But it was nothing:
the usual gang of students pushing through the desks to leave
the classroom as soon as possible, like every day, and the giggle
that followed was now their own business. He forgot
immediately, returned two chalk stubs to their box and wiped
the blackboard, leaving only the word "geodesics", underlined
twice, and finally even that disappeared under a whitish
residue. Eleven o'clock. He had time to walk back calmly.
But, on the pavement, the accusation and the giggle came back,
like a secret message, and he ran his hands over the top of his
head: yes, I need a haircut, he thought, and then without
thinking entered the *Unisex Hair Salon* that had opened two
blocks away from his home –in the past few days he had walked
past it and daydreamed about entering, about the futuristic
setting, those beautiful girls, that tall, androgynous, slim figure
managing the team with his spiky hair, all of it behind a window
that left the laboratory –it looked like a laboratory—exposed for
everyone to see.

He entered and immediately regretted it, faced by the smiling
black-clad figure that gave him no time to retreat and pointed
with a kind gesture, gently touching his shoulder, *this way*; and
it seemed like a trap, because there, in the brazenly modern

chairs –he recalled the designs from "The Jetsons", their floating, fluid and comical shapes—were two horrendous ladies, one with a white facial mask that looked like drying plaster, cracking around a pair of aggressive eyes and a hardened mouth, part woman part statue; and the other with hair painted in black tint that ran down her wrinkled forehead like an inky fringe, and both gave him accusing looks, gleaming, even furious, *what is that man doing here*, he imagined them thinking as he turned away, only to find a smiling girl with no makeup, possessed of a charm that was at once homely, transparent and absurd, like a happy schoolgirl, who pointed to one of the futuristic chairs, *Sit here, sir*, her arm extended. He almost slid off as he took a seat, once again feeling he was trapped, the chair leaning back like the ones at the dentist, and he imagined the cold light on the teeth, the scientist-like face assessing the damaged mouth, now the whole body tense, arms against the chair's armrests, the hands gripping tight, until the girl's fingers pulled up his neck with unexpected delicacy, fitting it into a rubber collar that weighed his head down –now he was staring straight at the white ceiling, drawing in his mind a map that connected the six –no, seven—randomly placed lamps, but he closed his eyes, giving in to the proceedings; with a careful adjustment, the girl's fingers retrieved the reluctant hairs still caught in the rubber collar, so that only his neck would remain there, but he should relax, the girl's face, now so close to his, seemed to be saying, *Are you comfortable, sir?*, a question that seemed truly interested in the answer, and he nodded a diminutive *yes* barely opening and closing his eyes, as if to avoid spoiling the lightness of the comfort brought about by the gentle and attentive voice –and he felt like the cape the girl was now unfolding covered him by the wind's force rather than by the agency of her hands, but he stopped thinking about it, eyes closed, waiting for the next step.

Without warning, save for a brief squeal that he did not even try to decipher, he felt the suddenness of the warm water filtering into his hair and with it the fingers that seemed to unravel it into separate strands, and he finally understood the use of the rubber collar around the neck, which stopped water from running down his body, kept things separate, the collar was a dyke between head and body, and he imagined a diagram on the blackboard, *tsunami*, he would say, drawing waves with the chalk –and now he felt the shampoo foam, the hair sliding through the fingers as if it were dripping, and when he heard *Is the temperature ok, sir?* he offered the same diminutive *yes* fearing that something would change in that moment of intense pleasure that made him hold his breath; more than the fingers (although them too), he felt the delicate touch of the nails, slow, drawing parallel lines on his hardened scalp (he smiled intimately at the image, which merely in being conjured seemed to open a new door in his life), the toughened skin, the subtle edge of the nails, the hands touching him with a total and innocent intimacy, causing spasms to spread across his body, twinges brief like –and again he pictured a diagram on the blackboard, the mental map of a naked and asexual body (but with an old-fashioned pointy moustache beneath the nose, as in a nineteenth century engraving, which made him laugh to himself again, that was funny, the lightness of the nails washing his hair), and trails leading from the root of every hair to some point on the body, like dotted aerial routes on a map or a scientific demonstration of the effects of acupuncture, in which he finally seemed to believe with some apprehension, like a doubting Thomas faced with concrete proof, the incredible

presence of those fingers and nails tangling in his hair with the dense foam and the warm water, here and there more intensely and slower, as if it were someone seeking a grain of sand, though never aggressively, building up to an epiphany that radiated through him like nothing he had ever felt in his life (a thought that almost deprived him of his current pleasure, like someone confronted by an obstacle made insurmountable by lack of precedents, an incomprehensible novelty), a pleasure that took over his entire body and then filled his soul, and which he would never dare take to its ultimate physical consequences, or simply the logical or obvious ones, such as, for instance—and he tried to remember the face of the girl washing his hair with such care, gentleness and wisdom, but he forgot, distracted by a fragment of melody that someone (perhaps even her, to judge from the sound's proximity) started whistling before falling silent again, and he was anxious to remember the lyrics to that popular piece of well-known music that now scurried away from him like an insect in the dark—now he could only hear a hair dryer in the next-door room, and the teacher thought that perhaps he was the reason for the silence, as if they were all reading his mind, as long as he was there life would be suspended in anticipation of his departure, but he had no time to feel anxious, because the girl shut off the water and replaced the pressure of the rubber collar with the softness of a towel protecting his neck, the delicate fingers pressing into the towel, so that his shirt wouldn't get wet. He seemed to wake up.
—Is that it?

She nodded, smiling, perhaps at the absurdity of the question, and took him to a room where the manager with spiky hair, cartoon-thin, waited with scissors in hand, also smiling, saying something he could not hear while the girl pulled the towel off him and covered him with another cape as he sat in a chair, upright this time, and then disappeared –he remained in front of the mirror, staring at himself starkly, the formless hair trickling down his head as if at the end of a party and he laughed to himself again. *I am Dinorei*, said the hairdresser, practical and polite, *How would you like your hair cut, sir?*, he asked, the comb carefully parting the hair at the top of the head, and the teacher pulled a face, almost tutting, *whatever*, he seemed to be saying, and that was really what he was thinking, whatever, all he wanted was to take with him the fingers and the nails and the foam and the warm water and the subtle web of touch that he did not want to lose, and he closed his eyes again. When he opened them, Dinorei was holding a small mirror behind his neck, left side, right side, left again, right again, so he could verify through that game of duplicate images the quality of the haircut, which was perfect, he concluded, getting up from the chair and putting his hand into his pocket to pay, already on his way out. It cost four times more than what he usually paid his old barber, but he didn't complain: he wanted to be on the street immediately, and once outside he felt the strange lightness of his head, his hair short like never before, as if his body were missing something –for a moment he tried to anticipate what the students would say. He took a few steps and unexpectedly remembered the lyrics to the interrupted whistling—

Beneath the curls
of your hair
—and further ahead crossed the road, entered the building, climbed the stairs and opened the door to his flat whistling the song but stuck on those two first verses lines as if they were an enigma that needed deciphering, the old vinyl record stuck

in a groove, *beneath the curls*, pause, *of your hair*, and then the emptiness of memory.

The woman, listening to the thread of his whistle, raised her eyes from the book she was reading when he entered the living room, adjusted her eyeglasses to see him in the distance, and smiled, either at the fragment of song or at his new haircut, but did not say the obvious thing he expected, *You cut your hair?*, or that perhaps she had thought of asking as she opened her lips, before something more urgent changed her line of thought:

–I left a plate ready for you in the microwave. I need to leave soon.– Her eyes went back to the book, which she closed immediately, in one sudden motion. –You took your time– she said, less as a complaint than stating a simple fact.

He felt a diffuse irritation. He sat in front of her and thought about saying, clearly, with the weight of a solemn announcement, or an eviscerated verse that has to be confessed, *Today I was touched like you never touched me* – but he kept quiet. Standing at the washbasin in front of the bathroom mirror he examined his hair, now with heightened attention, his almost aggressive fingers digging into it; *too short*, he murmured with a touch of distaste, calculating with a glimmer of hope how long it would be before he needed to return for another hair cut.

Calamares Campsite
Andréa del Fuego

I met Bolaño at a campsite on São Paulo's south coast. He was in charge of security, as if that were of any use. I paid the owner, Judite Calamares, up-front, and immediately noticed that the Chilean was sleeping with her. The eyeglasses, always greasy, intrigued me. If his vision was blurred with or without, why wear them? Today I understand. Bolaño does not want anyone to see his eyes, the globes yellowed by his liver, although this is less about aesthetics than about being Latin American. That way his gaze remains stripped bare, unconstrained, free of the obligation of seeing.

In May I told him I was pregnant, by August we were both living on the campsite, working as wardens. Judite Calamares spent her weekdays in the capital, buying mosquito netting and repellents, and visiting a relative in hospital. She returned before the weekend, carrying bags full of cheap tableware that she sold on to the fishermen's wives. Bolaño told me she sold Jamaican weed, I didn't believe it, but after I saw the fat cow spiking her fat customers' beers with a children's appetite stimulant, and ordering me to take the drinks, well. She spiked them right in front of me, and I realised, Judite Calamares sells Jamaican weed, but doesn't smoke, if she smoked she'd be sitting with the tourists wolfing down my pan-fried croquettes. It's a slippery slope once you cross that line.

Bolaño stared at the sea as if all that water could fit into a glass. I think the Jamaican weed had no effect on him, and, as he avoided drink because of his liver condition, he became the perfect night guard. Even though he dozed through the small hours, the wrinkle on his forehead still commanded people's respect.

When our son was born, Calamares said she was not going to support a family of wardens, and that if we planned to have another baby we should hit the road. We left that beach and stopped two parishes away, where Bolaño found work as cleaner in a hotel. No Jamaican weed, or disrespectful employer. I also found a way to get by, making crafts with seashells I collected in the morning, and I think that is how I started writing poems. When Bolaño read my first one, me on my fourth beer and he on his first Fanta, Bolaño thought he could do better and began writing poems during breaks in his cleaning job. I found it outrageous that he was so much better than me.

We decided to go to São Paulo, and we had only to set foot at Sé metro station to realise that we were going to go hungry. Bolaño didn't want to know about work, I had better luck and disposition, I found a job making photocopies and taking photos for official documents. The business was owned by Bolivians, but a group of middle-aged Chinese men sold clandestine products out of the backroom. The Chinese men played poker all day long and drank their booze. Bolaño came up with the idea of handing out our poetry with all the 3x4 photos, the Bolivians were unaware of it, customers would take our poetry away, folded next to their photographs. Small things, tiny handwriting on minuscule bits of paper. I'd appraise the customer first, if I thought he might appreciate the work he'd walk away with an unpublished poem.

One day my boss wanted a haircut and I volunteered, the most I had done with scissors until then was trim the photographs that our machine produced as if by magic. I pricked the Bolivian's nape, a Chinaman came out from the backroom and slapped me twice across the face when he saw the Bolivian bleed. At that stage Bolaño would stay at the hotel with our son writing poetry, feeding him bread and milk and eating nothing himself. When he saw my bruised cheekbone, he decided it would be better to return to Calamares Campsite.

Judite Calamares had already hired another warden, Bolaño said he could take care of other parts of the business. Jamaican weed does nothing to me, I smoked and didn't feel a thing. Bolaño decided to roll up the dope in my poems, while his own he treated with greater dignity, handing them over to buyers with their change. Before long, a student came back asking for more Jamaican weed, he became a regular client and volunteered to join the operation. One day, after Judite Calamares asked Bolaño to travel to the capital with her, to ensure her safety while out buying merchandise, I shacked up with the student for two whole days. He was out there camping for a week. I put my son to bed in Calamares' house and then spent myself from so much melting and screaming with that sensitive student who, after releasing my body on the shack's floor, read all of Bolaño's poems in a feigned voice. That stripling reading my husband's work after satiating my hunger excited me.

When Bolaño returned, the student told him everything. I knew what would happen, Bolaño was going to kill me, the fat cow was going to raise our child, the student would go home after a beating and Bolaño would grow old reclining on Calamares' belly. None of that happened. Bolaño wanted to know what poem the whippersnapper had read and they began discussing the poem's musicality. No one talked about the subject again, the student did not seek me out, it was as if he had to possess my body, because it belonged to the poet, before he could read the poem.

Six months later, when the two of them decided to travel to Peru on a whim, I stayed behind at Calamares Campsite. While I fried finger-food for the customers, my boy served the tourists fried calamari. It's been two years since I saw the Chilean's face, but I've received poems through the post, not very good ones, I admit. I think the student is impersonating him, Bolaño no longer writes to me.

Suli
Beatriz Bracher

1.

Meldor came to Brazil by orders of his father, Tarik Meltaya:
"in a fortnight you'll leave S., will go to Beirut and from there
to Brazil to bring back Herun Dulbi". S. was the village where
the Meltayas had lived and worked for generations. Herun
Dulbi was the first-born son of Najima Meltaya Dulbi, Tarik's
younger sister.

Najima was fourteen when she married Efrain Dulbi,
gave birth to one son and three daughters in the following five
years, and was a widow at nineteen. With four small children,
with no great dowry or appeal, she did not remarry. The father-
in-law, old Dulbi, was no longer alive, and her only brother-in-
law had migrated to Brazil. Faced with the nineteen-year-old
girl's sadness and disappointment, her mother-in-law allowed
her to return to S. taking even her boy, Herun, to educate him
there, after all she and her husband were cousins. They always,
always married among cousins. Tarik Meltaya, ten years older
than his sister, took care of her and his nephews as if they were
his own children.

Herun Dulbi had no memory of his father, but even so he
never full-heartedly accepted the shelter offered by his uncle.
He was a wary boy and given to mischief. While he was young
his mother protected him. From the age of seven his education

became his uncle's concern, and he was treated with the same severity as his cousins, sons of Tarik and Malake.

2. Herun

Herun was punished in the patio, in front of the whole family, cousins, uncles and even the women and servants, as if he were a child. This time Najima did not intercede, nor did she hide so her gaze did not add to her first-born's humiliation. Herun Meltaya Dulbi was accused of theft, and that broke her heart even more than seeing him get a thrashing. She stood there, eyes open, mouth closed even as she willed her son to accept and submit to the authority of Tarik, his dead father's arm and spirit.

Tarik Meltaya struck the boy Herun with forceful precision. The birds and the babies turned quiet. Through the mountain air, amid the smell of ripe berries, the only sound emerging from the patio with its sand and paving slabs was the whistle of the whip as it met the adolescent's flesh. Herun endured silently as red and disorderly lines appeared on his lean back. There was a pause, he turned to face his uncle and, in his voice that veered between masculine and feminine, said: "Tarik Meltaya, I'm Dulbi and you're a Meltaya, a chicken. Cluck-cluck-cluck." As he clucked the boy moved his arms like wings, tried to laugh, but his mouth, so beautiful it seemed almost a woman's, cried with hate and humiliation. Tarik Meltaya's rage, contained until now, expanded out of his body and he became a burning rod. The whip landed and left a mark on the boy's face, from his forehead to his jaw, and knocked him onto the ground. Herun, who was roguish but not a coward, rose from the earth like a mountain lion, only the light of his yellow eyes visible in his bloodied face, his skin goose-pimpled as a hump appeared to grow between his shoulders, thickening his upper body and his neck. But he was only fourteen and the uncle was not yet an old man.

Tarik threw the whip far away, took the nephew by the head with his bare hands with their short fingers and enormous palms, raised him up in the air until their eyes were level, and said: "I'm the spirit of your father, my cousin and friend Efrain Dulbi, repeat what you just said". Herun, baring his teeth, spoke with the deepest voice he could muster: "I stomp on the face of Tarik Meltaya, I spit in his food, I...", and before he was able to continue he found himself on the ground with broken teeth, blood running down his neck and chest. He got up and continued shouting: "this blood that stains your land is the tainted blood of the Meltayas. I have nothing that is yours, I have no mother". Najima let out a high-pitched cry, so high-pitched that it hurt the ears of all those who watched, stunned, as Tarik and Herun fought amid the mountain's silence, the berries and the patio. Tarik jumped onto his nephew, crouching on all fours over the boy who lay on the floor, holding him down by the wrists: "If Efrain were alive, he'd kill you. You are not a Meltaya, you are not a Dulbi." As he spoke, Tarik moved his body closer to his nephew's, as if wanting to crush Herun's hips with his weight, his teeth so close to the boy's face that everyone thought he would bite his nose off. Herun spat into his uncle's face. Tarik kept talking, shooting spittle into the nephew's mouth: "you're not even a camel, you're a girl". And then Tarik Meltaya got up, wiped his face and headed for the mountains.

That night, Herun did not sleep at home. Two weeks later Najima found out that her son had gone to Beirut and then made his way to Brazil. No one believed Herun would ever return, and they all thought he was right not to and gave thanks to God for having settled things in that manner. After all, nobody had died and Herun Dulbi had not had the time to drag the family into bigger trouble.

3. Najima

Najima stopped speaking. Her eyes did not make any accusations, nor did they possess the gleam of madness. Whoever saw Najima felt like crying. Hers was a face with no self-pity. She did not eat or speak, did not die or become ill, kept on working, cooking, cleaning, picking leaves from the berry bushes and taking them up into the mountains to feed the silkworms. She did not seek solitude, she carried it with her wherever she went. Najima's food made anyone who ate it sad, the silk produced by her insects was dark. Najima embodied lack and cold. Her family would have preferred her locked up in her room, wouldn't have minded working for her, cooking her food, washing her clothes, cleaning her room and even her body, no one would have minded praying for her health and paying whatever was necessary to Arab, English or French doctors. And they were not even rich.

But Najima Meltaya Dulbi did not become ill or seek consolation. She became thinner, she dried up, but carried on working even harder than before Herun Dulbi's departure. It was not by force of rancour or bitterness, it was not accusations of guilt that accompanied her everywhere she went. Sadness and a will to die took hold of the house.

Since his aunt Najima had fallen mute, Meldor knew that one of his father's sons would have to go and find Herun Dulbi, wherever he was, but did not expect to be the chosen one. Only four years ago he had married his cousin Suli Meltaya, of the Henoti Meltayas, they had a boy and a girl, Farid and Nejme, and she was pregnant with her third child. Now he had a fortnight to get ready for his journey.

4. Najima's death

Tarik noticed immediately after Meldor's departure for Brazil that Najima, unhappy Najima, did not ever want her son back. In her heart, Herun had become a sick boy when he stole at the card game in Istiba and had died when he repudiated his mother in the house of her brother and protector, Tarik Meltaya, in front of the family and the servants. The son's homecoming would be the return of a ghost that was young and beautiful, like he always was, or old and ugly, like he would never become, but whether this one or that one it would be a body whose likeness with someone she loved and who broke her heart would only cause pain.

When Tarik's house became happy again, even despite his melancholy singing, when, after Herun's departure, a third merchants' caravan with its camels camped outside the family home and the youngsters laughed again with the foreigners' tales, and Tarik Meltaya himself was once again telling his own tales filled with wonder and terror, when that night arrived, Najima Meltaya Dulbi woke up in the dark moaning softly. At sunrise she got up and started working and carrying out the tasks that she had never stopped doing, but everyone could see that she was in a lot of pain and her moan, even if her mouth was closed, could be heard far away. At the end of the day she fell on the ground holding her head as if she wanted to rip it off.

The women took her to a dark room far away from the noise, they tried rags soaked in cold water and hot water. They tried infusions that she refused and, when they insisted, she vomited. Najima spent the night moaning, keeping the family awake, as they waited for the poor woman's head to blow up, because her moan was like the whistle of a boiling pot, ready to explode. The following morning they called the doctor, who could do nothing to alleviate the woman's pain. By the third day Tarik Meltaya's sister looked grey and ten years older than the century she had aged since the departure of her first-born son. Inside the dark room, Najima closed her eyes hard, bit the sheets and covered her ears with her hands. Her muted moan reached ever further and the children began dreaming of mutilations and murders.

Malake Meltaya, Tarik's cousin and wife, Najima's sister-in-law, in desperation at her friend's pain, had the unfortunate idea of calling Istiba's priest. When Father Abdula arrived in S., the whole village was waiting, because Efrain's widow's moans reached as far as the last house in the village and up the mountainside. The man with the long and filthy beard asked to be left alone with the insane woman, as he called her. This was not possible even if he was a priest and Najima was a woman beyond age. Malake stayed with them and witnessed her friend's final hell, and the Maronite man's last sigh. The priest lit candles in the closed room and began reciting his litany. Najima's moan became a howl. The man of God prayed faster and louder, walked with deliberate heaviness around Najima, swinging the incense-burner as it filled the room with its smoke and its odour. Poor Najima Meltaya Dulbi. Malake later told of how her sister-in-law leaped onto Father Abdula with nails and teeth at the ready. For Najima, who had been shrivelled for three days, the effort of stretching herself out again was such that something inside her ripped. Her eyes bulged and her mouth snapped shut around the priest's neck. They both fell over and the sound of Najima's head hitting the ground was the last thing heard by those waiting outside.

When they opened the door, they found Malake crouching and trying to save those who had no salvation, Najima with her eyes open, nails piercing the priest's eyes and her mouth clamped shut on his jugular. A thick trickle of the Father's blood ran out the side of Najima's mouth and once again sullied Tarik Meltaya's house.

5. Suli

Najima died. Let the name of Herun Dulbi never darken any place where a Meltaya might be. Meldor was to return to Lebanon, to S., to take care of his family. Melchior Meltaia (as he was now known in Brazil) sent money year after year so that his wife Suli and the children could join him in Brazil. Year after year, his father Tarik kept the money. Suli and Meldor's children grew up under their grandfather's protection. Suli was a good daughter-in-law, she helped Malake until the end of her life, cooking and cleaning her house with dedication and affection. Obedient to her father-in-law, she never tried persuading him to listen to her husband's pleas and allow her to join him in Brazil with her children. Nor did she ever reproach her husband for not coming back to his family. She knew that if Meldor returned to S. Tarik would never let him leave again, and she wanted to leave some day. Deep down in her heart, Suli wanted to know a land that was larger than S.

6. Brazil

When she was shown her house, on the main square of a small town in Minas Gerais, Suli walked around her husband's ground-floor shop, climbed the staircase and found she liked the rooms and the first-floor living area. The chickens were scratching the earth in the back yard and the vegetable patch was well tended. Suli walked around the building once again. She asked her husband where the oven for baking bread was. Tarik explained that things were different in Brazil, bread was not baked at home. No one ate bread at the Meltaya family's house until a clay oven was built in the back yard. Suli explained to her husband that her children would not eat bread kneaded by another woman's hands.

Once a month, Djalma, the son born in Brazil, the one who, aged eight, translated Portuguese for his mother and Arabic for her customers, walked to the police cell with short but decisive steps, his chubby legs sticking out of the shorts sewn by his mother, to deliver pita bread for the prisoners. One of Suli's ways of expressing her gratitude for that land larger than S.

Princes' Manor
Marcelino Freire

Four black men and one black woman stopped in front of this building.

The first thing the porter said was: "Good God!" The second: "What do you want?" or "Which apartment?" Or "Why haven't you fixed the service lift yet?"

"We're making a film," we reply.

Caroline added: "A documentary." Whatever that means, beats me, I dunno. Let's just show him our IDs and we're ready to go.

"We're filming."

Filming. That's what criminals do when they're going to kidnap someone. They observe the daily life, the habits, what time the victim goes to work. There are bank managers in this building, doctors, lawyers. And of course the building's administrator. The administrator is never in.

—Where are you from?

—From Pavão Hill.

—We've come to shoot a feature-length documentary.

—Shoot what?

Shooting, long-barrel guns, grenades, black guys armed to the teeth. Didn't I say there'd be trouble? I'm outta here. North-easterners are real men. The porter, is he or isn't he a real man? Caroline was saying: "Our plan is to enter one of this building's apartments, unannounced, and to start filming, do an interview with the resident."

The porter: "Enter an apartment?"

The porter: "No."

Thinking: "I'm fucked."

It was my idea, I confess. People keep coming up our hill
to make films. We open our doors, show them our pots and pans,
our shit.

This is how it happened: I bought a third-hand camera,
we met, we rehearsed a few times. Exclusive images, taken
from the life of the middle class.

Caroline: "Come on, darling, please." From far away,
Caroline showed him the microphone. She waved with her
lipstick, who knows what she was doing.

Am I going to be beaten with a microphone? The microphone
was borrowed from a spirit medium who sponsored us.

The porter buzzed apartments 101, 102, 108. He buzzed
every floor. I'm being mugged, coerced, call 190, or whatever.

The point was that no one should know. Otherwise the
interview loses its spontaneity. The resident speaking about
what it's like to live with cars in the garage, bills to pay,
swimming pool, a networked computer. Money and success.
Brasilia Film Festival. Gramado Film Festival. Screening our
film at school, in this building's recreation room.

No.

We don't just listen to samba. We don't just hear gunshots.
This porter doesn't even behave like a black man, keeping us
locked out. Our hill is up there, open twenty-four hours a day.
We welcome people with open hearts. The bastards come,
meddle in our past. We lay ourselves bare for them like tame
birds. We unload our thoughts like parrots. We sing, we sway.
We offer them our Coca-Colas.

That goddamned porter won't let us start. It's fucked up. Sunday, today's Sunday. We just want to know how the family has lunch. If they have the same habits as we do. Plate, feijoada, napkin. Come on, you don't have to call the administrator. Just listen. We're going to get the camera out of the bag. We're going to show you that we come in peace, we just want to improve our chances. Make films. Movies. Look at Fernanda Montenegro, she almost won an Oscar.

—No, Fernanda Montenegro doesn't live here.

And then he told us: "I'm calling the police."

No one likes the police. We don't want to appear in that kind of news clip. We made some big fucking sacrifices to get this far. Nicholson didn't go selling his sweet dough fritters. Caroline gave up her clubbing. I left my wife, my dog and my son at home. No, it won't even be a full-length film, just a short one. A poor man's happiness is tough. Start filming. What? I gave the order: Start filming.

We filmed everything. Some residents sticking their heads out on balconies. The passing traffic. The police siren. Huh? The police siren. Every film has a police siren. And gunfire. Lots of gunfire.

Violence on camera. Shit, Jonathan jumped over the wrought iron fence. The porter locked himself in his glass cabin. Terrifying. All sorts of people showed up. And that wasn't the plan. We had to improvise.

Fine, no worries.

We'll cut it out in the edit.

Thorn
João Anzanello Carrascoza

In the beginning was the silence of the hills, some made of stone, others tufted with grass, and I couldn't see very far, my eyes too small to take in such vastness. But, as if he knew more about me than I did, André was there, to help me. And I could see more if he was nearby, even as we crossed through maize fields, when we went to São Tomé lake, the dry foliage choking the path, and, suddenly, with his voice less child-like than mine, he would say, *Look, the maize is out*, and I saw it, in the rebound of discovery, and then him, *Pull forward*, teaching me how to harvest– the unexpected happiness.

We arrived at São Tomé, the calm lake, the diminutive trees on its shores, the mountain range in the distance, endless, layered, my gaze unable to take in that beauty, and André, sitting on the large rock, would say, *First you have to see it all at once*. So I'd fix my eyes on the horizon, and, *Then*, he would add, *then you look at each thing*, an invitation to examine the details. And so I forgot myself, pictured myself on the blue-hued mountains, saw the ipê tree that rises by the farm's big house, the thread of chimney smoke, a cloud's white wisp, the pebbles in front of us, and at last, as my eyes came to rest on them, my feet.

My brother and I, our gazes always coming and going. It was good to play with him, or to do whatever Father asked –fix the fence, sweep the patio, collect lemongrass. *Come, help me*, André said. He liked company, even the dogs', Deco and Lilau, and he went about completing his tasks, engrossed. I remember the time when we were building a trap, squatting on the beaten earth, and he stood up and said, *Look, look,* and I raised my eyes – it was the blue sky over our heads, so lovely! The everyday sky, but looking different, the sky that made us weightless in its flow.

With André the world revealed itself in novelties, the world was awake, and days, any and every one of them, were days for remembering what the eyes forgot amid the habit of seeing too much, like the morning when Aunt Tereza came to visit. We had gone out to the pastures, and there the cows wandered, ruminating among the termite mounds, and the sun was coming out behind the hills, parakeets leaving their noisy trail in the air, André wishing to grow up, *To ride Father's horse, help him with the calves!* We saw mother come out onto the veranda and, even though we were far away, my brother said, *Did you see that? Mother is happy,* and I said, *To me she always seems the same,* and he, *It's a different kind of happiness.* We went home, in a hurry, and already from the staircase we could hear the talking, the familiar laugh, and, there in the kitchen, Aunt Tereza; she came so rarely, but how good her presence was for Mother, they must have been like André and me when they were children. And I wanted to grow up and buy a farm beyond the mountain range and return one day, just like Mother and Aunt Tereza, to see my brother, and the two of us grown up, and doing new things.

That was our time, when we were children, and I understood less of everything, and he helped me to see more. André was, at certain times, like Father and Mother, well-informed, full of knowledge: he knew, just by observing the stars, if it was going to rain; he could tell if a bird in the branches of a tree was a sanhaço, a tuim or a kingfisher; he predicted, correctly, what week the harvest would start at São Tomé. And he invented things that made us laugh, like saying who people resembled, a little game of ours that no one else knew about: *Father? Father looks like the midday sun, strong...And Mother? Mother has eyes like a jabuticaba. And Aunt Tereza? Aunt Tereza is the noisiest of parrots! And cowboy João? Look at him carefully, cowboy João has the face of an armadillo. And the dogs, André? Deco. Deco is like a big fat toad. And Lilau? Lilau looks like Zita the Healer. And Zita the Healer? Zita looks like Lilau.* And we laughed, we laughed, life slipping by...

I liked those gentle hours, it was like entering São Tomé lake without sinking, staying in its calm shallow waters, free of danger. But there were other times when my heart shrank, at day's end, the room's darkness. And André was with me: *You can sleep, I'm here,* he said, and he was. Because whenever I asked, *Are you awake, André,* he replied, *I am,* and reassured me, *Now sleep,* and I prayed quietly, and the Guardian Angel, who I saw when I closed my eyes, had his face. And dreams came, mixed fragments of things that happened, sometimes an entirely new story, me in the fields with Father, then taking care of cows with cowboy João, and it was almost like a real day, even Deco and Lilau were in the dreams, curling themselves around our legs, and, suddenly, as in the waking hours, I helped André saddle Father's horse, and off he went, galloping, towards the stone hills, getting smaller and smaller until, amid the green of the range, he seemed like speck in the landscape. But, when I opened my eyes, he reappeared, as if happy from his trip through my dream, and he called to me, *Come on, the sun is rising,* the morning spreading over everything, illuminating the fields, the morning like the one I saw in my sleep. We got up without anyone calling us, like birds, in the happiness of flight, and like the cows and the calves and the horses, all standing, that is how they slept, because, upon waking up, they were ready, the world beginning anew.

But lurking in those hours, like a snake in the grass, was evil, biding its time, and then, when we weren't looking, jumping out from its hiding place, and when it came, it was as if, instead of the day beginning, night fell, a night with no stars, not even fireflies, or crickets, night that hurt like a thorn in the foot.

News came that Zico, the son of Seu Manuel, São Tomé's owner, had drowned in the lake. Father knew him, had been at his christening, a celebration that had required several whole beef carcasses on a spit-roast, musicians from the town, no expenses spared, it was Seu Manuel's big day. The party, Father said, had taken place on the lake's shore, just the other day he was remembering it, because it had been unusual, the neighbouring families all coming together to celebrate, but then he abruptly stopped talking, as if he were lingering over other memories. Mother said, crying, *He could have been one of my children*, and she hugged us, *You mustn't go to São Tomé again, you understand?*, even Deco and Lilau were acting strange, as if they knew things.

The storm came, the kind that takes shape casually between clouds, and before you know it, and even if it's still daytime, has darkened the horizon, and its rain and its wind wrecked everything in our sight – the stable tiles, the electricity post knocked over, the mire outside our door, and the saddest thing: lightning had killed two calves that Father was going to sell for Christmas. When the rain cleared, as quickly as it had arrived, we went to see its damage at close range: cowboy João used a bamboo stick to poke one of the calves, which remained inert, as if it were sleeping on the grass; Father sad, amid his astonishment.

And there was the time of the burglary at Aunt Tereza's house. She lived on the Água Rasa ranch, beyond the rocky range, a place that mother described as lovely, with pools of water mirroring the sky above –reflecting the sun, the birds, nature up high–, but close to a road with a lot of traffic. Aunt Tereza had gone into town for some shopping with Uncle Alceu and, when they returned, before entering the ranch, she recognized some of her possessions strewn around: clothes, pillows, pots. Inside the house, chaos; almost everything, including the statue of Our Lady, had disappeared. Aunt Tereza suffered; when she came to tell Mother, she was beyond herself. But as she left she said something remarkable: she had nothing left to lose, and it was good not to have things, because we become unhappy about them, we fear losing them. Now she could be truly happy, and she laughed, and was again Aunt Tereza.

Other stories made us feel alive: André came running from the pastures, Deco trailing him, and said, *There's a circus in town, Father is taking us.* The two of us were on the veranda in an upheaval of happiness, inventing our own circus, and the grass in its silence seemed a lovelier shade of green. Father's ranch, too, suddenly appeared to welcome every day with a new satisfaction, there was something different about things, something that I couldn't explain, but it was there, everything was the same but stronger, Mother even hummed songs, and then, André stopped near a flower bed, *Look at that!* And I saw what I hadn't seen, despite being right there: the roses flowering, the lilies, the daisies. I understood: it was Spring. The trees standing there, as always, but so full of life, almost bursting, like seeds, and the birds flew and chirruped even more, and Deco and Lilau ran here and there barking loudly, I sensed the differences but couldn't tell there were differences, and to discover them like that with André gave me a wonderful sort of fright, and then new yearnings took over me, *I'm going to get a rose for Mother...*

And without Mother knowing, one day we went back to São Tomé lake and sat on the big boulder to watch the mountain range. André wanted to get into the water, *Come,* and I went, and we got in. He swam out to the middle and waved back at me on the shore, under the trees' shade, and I remembered Seu Manuel, my heart aching; in that place where we were happy, Zico had died.

The next day I woke up before my brother, he was breathing loudly. I called, *Let's go, the sun is out!,* and he grumbled, wanted to sleep. Mother worried, put her hand on his forehead. *He's burning.* She made tea and said, *Stay here with him,* both of us in the bedroom, an unusual event, we were not accustomed to being indoors, we belonged outside. André tried to get up, he couldn't, then he said, *Help me, open the window,* and I opened it, and we saw –the blue mountains seen from the room's compactness, hungry to grow, to regain their real magnitude.

André refused his lunch, *I'm not hungry, Mother,* he was nauseous, unusually tired. In the afternoon, Father went to find Zita the Healer, Zita who looked like Lilau; I perked up when she arrived, André, were he not ill, would have looked at me, in that way of his, and I would have laughed with him, about our game. Zita prayed, assured us of his recovery and left. But, in the depths of night, André moaned, he trembled, *It's cold, it's very cold, Mother,* he mumbled strange things, about cowboy João, the circus, the ipê tree at São Tomé, he mixed recollections and inventions.

As soon as the sun came out, Father prepared the horse-cart to take André into town, Lilau and Deco barking all the way to the gate, me and Mother watching from the veranda, wanting desperately to pull out that thorn. I wanted the world to be a good place, and I could imagine Father coming back with André, us living our lives again, with things to do, without the bad frights. Father came back mid-afternoon with Aunt Tereza. She and Mother hugged without smiles or silliness, Aunt Tereza was someone else, something was missing, André would have said, in that noisiest of parrots. She was coming to take care of me and the house, Mother was going to spend the night at the hospital with Father.

Mother did not return the following day, or the ones after, only Father came back every morning, to take care of the fields and the cattle with cowboy João. Aunt Tereza said André would be fine, I would visit him soon, Uncle Alceu would take the two of us to the circus. I closed my eyes and saw my brother, smiling on the horse-cart, between Father and Mother, and from wanting it so much he appeared to me often, and every time he called out, *Let's go play, I recovered,* and he'd run out to the pastures, *Let's help Father with the calves.* But André was taking long. Time passed painfully. Even more so when I opened the window onto the landscape and remembered his words: *First you have to see it all at once. Then, then you look at each thing...*

So it went, until one morning, when Aunt Tereza and I were in the kitchen, and Mother entered the house with her eyes full of sleep, Father next to her, tied up by silence. Deco and Lilau came in after them and curled up at their feet, unceremoniously. Mother lowered her head. Father took her hands in his: they were crying. It was the start of our yearning. I walked out through the back of the house, my gaze trying to take slow flight. I saw the stone hills in the distance, the grass growing on their flanks, the blue mountains. Without André, who would help me to see that vastness?

Neighbours
Ferréz

It took a while to get all the money together, I was down to just
one pair of trainers and two shorts. Paying for the house was
difficult, I had to bulk-buy my shirts at Bresser, plain white,
at three reais and ninety cents each, in packs of no less than ten,
the only way to save.

It didn't matter, I wanted to move, my neighbours had pushed
me to the brink. I had spent a whole month chasing that dark-
skinned beauty, she had slept with me, we had a good fuck –
even though the buses that rushed past made my room tremble.
But back to the subject, after we finally got round to it, came the
setback: the moment I came out of my room with her, a bearded
neighbour (damn him) saw us and said:

—Ha! Look at you all sweaty.

She never looked at me again.

Another thing I couldn't stand any longer was that my
bedroom window looked straight out onto four windows
belonging to the worst families. A woman with frazzled hair
leaned against one of them all day long. When her husband
arrived she would leave for an hour and then come back,
and spent the rest of the afternoon staring at my room.

Once I got up early in the morning and, too lazy to go
downstairs to use the toilet, decided to have a piss in the
stairwell. As soon as I started relieving myself, I noticed
someone opening a window, I couldn't believe it, she was

staring, I couldn't stop pissing, it felt so good. So, as soon as I finished, I grabbed my cock in my left hand and turned towards her and started shaking it. I was very sleepy, but I could swear I noticed the expression on her face changing, and then she stepped away from the window.

At night there were always people calling out for me, the kind of friends who stay in your house drinking coffee until the early hours. But every time, before I could open my window, I heard others opening, it was them, they were spying, perhaps they thought me and my friends would smoke a joint, or whatever, and I was worried they'd think we were bum buddies. So I no longer opened my window, and my friends stopped coming.

I slammed the door many times on my neighbours. Whenever I arrived carrying a bag they wouldn't stop staring at it, trying to figure out what was inside. When I rented porn films, I asked the boy from the rental place to double-bag them, but I knew they could still see through them, because the boxes for porn films were red and the bags were very thin.

The neighbour on the left had a dog that wouldn't stop barking for a second, I could no longer sleep, his barks echoed in my head. I decided to buy some poison, but when I got home I realised my mistake: the guy from the bar who sold me the poison was an acquaintance of hers, if the dog was poisoned I could be blamed.

I was scared, very scared, nothing seemed to shock them, I grew tired of the gross things going on all the time, when these people got angry they said the worst things, I might wake up to shouts of —You and your shrivelled cock, you haven't fucked me for a month—or phrases such as –But darling, my daughter, he came over to fuck me, I never went over there to give it up to him.

Back then I tolerated the loud music played by the neighbour on the right, I learned all the songs by Zezé di Camargo and Luciano, and when I bought some shelving at Marabraz I gave her the free wall-clock, I'd never seen such a gentle smile.

But two days later I was certain she was going crazy, that woman had always spread gossip about my family, and last year she had told everyone I was definitely a poof, which is what I hate the most. According to her, no one who calls himself a man spends so much time studying in his room.

Once I had all the money I visited the estate agents, I didn't want to move to a new neighbourhood, I liked that one, I just couldn't stand the neighbours. Tramps and whores, I had trouble with every one of them. I found many nice houses, but they were all expensive, I looked around for over three months. And, during that time, I threatened to kill the neighbour from across the street: he was always staring at my mouth while I talked to my friends, I know he was reading my lips.

I was sure he wanted to know what I was saying, I couldn't resist giving him the finger that Wednesday afternoon. I thought about putting him in my new novel, but gave up: I was not going to immortalise him.

Finally I found one, it had all sorts of plants growing in the large back yard, and it was only a couple of blocks away from my mother, the price was good, it was cheaper because of the nearby brook. I didn't mind that small detail, I could clean up the mud whenever the brook flooded, I could clean it all every day as long as no one was trying to read my lips or find out what films I had in my bags.

I went to see the house one last time to be certain, it was Friday, birds flew in and out all the time. I went out to the garden.

You couldn't see the street from within, good. The neighbour on one side lived far away, there was only an empty lot. On the other side lived one of my mother's cousins, she had separated from her husband and had two girls who kept the volume down when they listened to music.

I also gave thanks to God for the neighbour at the back: there was a large barn in which an evangelical church had set up its operations. They had services only on Saturdays –I could live with that, nothing is perfect.

I dried my mother's tears, took my books and moved house. Months later, the empty lot next door was rented out for a sort of recycling yard, but I became accustomed to the sound of a machine pressing plastic bottles, though I was still startled by the noise it made when it crushed tin cans.

I had an argument with the next-door neighbour, my mother's cousin: she built a wood-fire stove, right next to the dividing wall, that filled my house with smoke every day. I tried to say that wasn't right, she threatened to call the police and told everyone on the block that I was a thief, that the whole writing thing was a lie.

The church behind my house increased the length of its services, and I now knew who Moses was, and the Apostle Paul, and why the Psalms matter.

Around that time, one morning, I went out for bread and, when I opened my front gate, noticed for the first time the piles of rubbish that people were dumping by the brook. I tried not to think about it, I walked slowly to the bakery and on the way came across a lame dog. I stopped to pat it on the head, and that big son of a bitch tried to bite me.

I went back home, thinking about making myself some coffee, but I'd run out of cooking gas, so I decided to go for a walk:

I went to the nearest (and only) park and ran for forty minutes. Later I sat on a bench for another thirty, trying to rid myself of the image of a roast chicken that came into my head from the moment I started running.

I went back home and noticed a blue Uno parked in front of my gate—some impertinent moron. At least the recycling yard had stopped crushing plastic bottles (the next day they'd be breaking glass bottles against the wall, one day a piece of glass came flying over and almost hit my head, in the morning I'd find my back yard full of pieces of glass, but that was a minor quibble, I won't get worked up about it).

The church started its service just as I was planning to have a wank, forget it.

They'd extended their schedules and now, besides rehearsing every day, they also had daily services, I knew all their prayers, I decided to take a nap.

The other day I woke up early, the car was still there but I noticed that its side-windows were broken, that's when I realised it must be stolen. I called the police many times, the day went by and nobody came. At night I was disturbed by rats scratching the bedroom's false ceiling, their nails gave me goose flesh, but I finally managed to sleep around four in the morning –the recycling yard started breaking glass bottles at seven.

I went out for bread and, when I opened my front gate, noticed a white car abandoned against my wall. Just what I needed, the front of my house had become a bone-yard. I left the bread at home, decided to visit my old address, and when I strolled down the old street and saw my old neighbours I felt like saying hello to them, they didn't seems quite as bad any more. The street had a slight inclination and tears came to my eyes when I realised for the first time that my old home did not have a recycling yard next door, nor did it have a church at the back, and had never had rats.

But it was too late to go back: the house was mine and that was my fate. So, when I was back at my front gate, I glanced over at the blue Uno and saw that it had some nice looking black seats and noticed its stylish steering wheel. I was never into cars, but I decided I wanted that steering wheel in case I ever had a car. So I got into the Uno and started pulling, I realised it was going to be difficult. So I went into the house to get a screwdriver and a hammer.

A few minutes later I had managed to pull off the steering wheel, and started eyeing the gear-knob: it had a nice picture of a crab. As I yanked it off, I heard the siren. I tried to explain, but the steering wheel was on my lap. The policemen I called had finally arrived.

Some neighbours testified in court, but they all said I was new on the street and that there had never been any stolen cars before I moved in.

The owner of the recycling yard was in court, so too were some people from the church, and to this day I haven't understood when I was sentenced.

I'm now in a very quiet place. The only problem is having to share the toilet and sometimes having to sleep on the floor, whenever I lose the draw and have to hand my bed over to some cellmate.

God is Good
André Sant'Anna

For Pati

When I liked football, I supported Corinthians. But now I know that football isn't Godly. Players get things mixed up. How can God make Marcelinho score a goal? If God were helping a team to win its games, that team would never lose. If Corinthians were God, Corinthians would win every game. And doesn't Corinthians lose? Marcelinho keeps saying it's God that scores the goals. But it isn't God. It's Marcelinho himself, no one else. Other teams also have players who say God scores their goals. So, where does that leave us? God cannot be a supporter and score for every team. Even God can't do that, you can only have one team, choose one and that's it. You'd never catch God switching sides, because he has only one Word, and that is the true Word. If God scored goals for every team with a player who claims God scores goals, everything would end in a draw. That's why football has no God. That's why football is not Godly. So, when we love Marcelinho, or when we love Corinthians,
we don't love God. God doesn't like it when people love a football team instead of loving God. The only love we can feel is for God. The only love we can feel is for Jesus, who is God himself, and the Holy Ghost, who is a mystery to me, but is also God. Some people believe the Holy Ghost is that dove. But the Holy Ghost is no dove. It's God. So, people have to love God, who is the father, though not Joseph, who is also the father, but

different, not the proper father, because only God is the father. We have to love Jesus, born unto his father, Joseph, who is not God, and unto the father who is God, and is the same as Jesus. Because Jesus is Jesus, the son, and is also God. He is his own father, God, but also has two fathers: Joseph, who is not God, and God, who is also the son. And then there's the Holy Ghost. We also have to love the Holy Ghost, which is God in the shape of a dove. Because God is three people, but is one and the same, God himself, who is different from Joseph, but is also the father, and is also Jesus Christ, who is the son and is his own father at the same time, and the Holy Ghost, which is not a dove and is also God. We shouldn't love or like anything else. Not even the national team, Brazil, and we shouldn't believe that lie about God being Brazilian, because God is God for the whole world and Jesus, the son of God and also God himself, was born in Bethlehem, which is different from the city of Belém here in Brazil. That other Bethlehem is the one with the Jews and with Bin Laden shooting and saying that their god is the God, but he isn't God, he's not even the Holy Ghost, he's just a crazy excuse for terrorism because they are envious of God, who is the same God they have over there in the United States, the God who is Jesus, the one God for the whole world. So we mustn't love Brazil, which is just a football team, though bigger than Corinthians, and with players from all teams. And when they win the Cup it's even worse, because then players lift it like it was an idol and God commanded us not to worship idols. And the cup is golden like the golden lamb that God commanded Moses not to worship, because Moses is not God, he is the prophet who arrived in Egypt to kill those people who worshipped the golden lamb. God doesn't like us to worship anything golden, no sir. You can't love gold cups, no sir.

You can't love anything that isn't God. We mustn't even love our own wives too much. Women cause lust, and that's why I don't even look at women. When we do, we're filled with lust and we forget to love God. Even Mary, Our Lady, we mustn't love her, because she's a woman and is not God. God is a man called Jesus and is the father but isn't Joseph and is the Holy Ghost that is a dove but is also God. The Holy Ghost made Mary, Our Lady, who isn't God, pregnant with Jesus, who is God. That's why the Holy Ghost is also a man, and is God, because God is the father of Jesus, who is God, but without having any sex. We can only love God the man. Except that God is not a man, because he is God. Only his sex makes God a man. But not sex of the kind you have with a woman. I mean sex as that thing in a document that says a person is male or female. God is male, but he is God and not one of those male men who like women. God doesn't like sex and that's why he sent the Holy Ghost to have sex with Mary, Our Lady, because he, God himself, doesn't like women. And someone had to make Jesus inside the belly of Mary, Our Lady. But the sex that the Holy Spirit had with Mary, Our Lady, who is not God, is a different kind of sex, more like a gust of air, or a light that enters Our Lady' belly, so they didn't need to have sex, of the sort I used to enjoy before I loved God and, now that I don't love women, only God, I don't enjoy any more, because God is against that kind of sex. God is against women, against football, against drinking, against cigarettes, against television. God is against all those things that are good, because everything that's good is bad because it makes us forget about loving God. People only remember God when something bad happens, that's why we need bad things to happen all the time, so we'll remember God all the time. God does not like us to forget about loving him. God doesn't even like us to laugh a lot. Because laughing a lot is a sign that we're enjoying something that isn't God. When we love God, we love him seriously, no laughing. That's why now I'm always serious and I'm not laughing and I love God with a straight face. I love God and I suffer because God likes that. God likes us to be in agony so we can see how good it is to feel the same agony that Jesus, who is God, felt up on the cross. That's a good agony. God likes that agony. Because when we feel that agony, we pay for our sins, even if we didn't do anything, because sin is born with us because Adam had sex with Eve after he ate the apple. That's why God doesn't like women –because Eve gave Adam the apple to eat and Adam wanted to have sex, which God does not like. And it led to this: now we have to be in agony. But our agony, because we're not God, isn't as great as that of Jesus, who is God. That's why we must be serious and suffer a lot, to feel at least a part of the suffering felt by Jesus, who is God. Do you think it's easy to serve God? It isn't. To serve God, we can't be hanging around bars, drinking beer, checking out women and talking about football and politics. I hate politics. God doesn't like politics, or those people who are always complaining about the government. I never complain about anything, because complaining is the same as liking something. We complain when something interferes with those things we like. And God doesn't like us to like something other than God. So nowadays I don't complain about anything because these days I don't like anything. Only God. I won't ever like anything else, that's why I hate politics, especially when it's the politics of being against things, which means complaining, which means liking things that aren't God. Those who are against everything want the government to do good things for them and forget that, if the government does only good things, they won't feel the agony that is so bad, but which is good because it makes God like us. Those who are against everything just want the government to do good things for them and forget the bad things that God does for their own good and also to take revenge on Adam who, instead of loving God, spent his time in Eder having sex, eating apples and liking Eve, stark naked all day long. Not me. I won't ever like anything again. Not even my wife, who I am marrying next month. I swear. No, I won't swear, because God doesn't like us to swear, it's taking his name in vain. I promise I won't love my wife very much. The minute I realise I'm loving my wife too much I'll stop loving her. Whenever I feel the desire to love my wife, all I have to do is think of God and the Holy Spirit who isn't a dove, it's God. And so we stop loving everything else and love only God, who is the only thing that we can love. You can love thy neighbour too if he's not a woman, or football, or anything that you mustn't love, or that God doesn't like. We need to love our neighbours too, but without getting carried away. You have to love thy neighbour but not too much, because you shouldn't love thy neighbour more than you love God. God is much better than thy neighbour, that's why above all else we must love God. Neighbours come later, because God comes first. First God, then Jesus, who is also God, then the Holy Ghost, who looks like a dove, but is God, then thy neighbour and, finally, all the way down there close to hell, which does exist, comes sex, which is the worst thing, the thing that God likes least of all. That's why I won't have too much sex with the woman I'll be marrying next month. Only twice, because I want to have two children, a boy and a girl, who won't be able to like anything, only God. I'll make my children love God from an early age so they'll grow up being used to it. After they learn to walk and talk they'll have to start suffering, because when God makes children become grownups they start wondering whether there is a God. And my children must grow up believing there is a God. I'll show them there is a God. To give them the right upbringing, we have to be even stricter with them than God is with us. We have to make our children suffer, feel pain, and that way they'll learn to love God. The girl won't even go to school so she won't ever want to have sex. The boy can go, because he's a male and has to learn a little bit about having sex so he can grow up and go forth and multiply, which is what God commanded. At science lessons at school they teach that thing about the uterus, the sperm, and how children are born. God allows us to have sex so we can make children. As long as we don't enjoy it. I won't enjoy sex because God is completely against sex. My son won't enjoy sex either. My son will only have sex to go forth and multiply. God only wants us to love him. If we love God and don't laugh too much, then later, when we die, we'll be able to do everything and enjoy the things we do. And so I'll cheer for Corinthians again and I'll drink beer, because I don't like drinking now, but I'll enjoy it when I die. I'll even love my wife after she's died. I'll enjoy my wife after I die and after she dies. My wife and I will have lots of sex when we're dead. When you're dead, it's okay. I can even have sex with other women after I've died and after they've died. When we're dead, it's okay. Except there won't be lots of women to have sex with, because women who have sex don't go where I'm going, up there in Eder, because women who have sex are very pretty and God doesn't like pretty women. What God likes is ugly women, fat women, hairy women with varicose veins. God likes those women that don't make us want to have sex with them. But I won't be having sex with those horrible women, because I'll be dead and I won't have to like things that aren't good. But I'll be able to have sex with the woman who'll be my wife a month from now, because now she'll let herself become ugly so we can have sex with each other when we both die. Up there, in Eder, she'll be pretty. There, she's allowed to. Up there in Eder –which sounds like the name of that bad-tempered football player, Éder, but is also the name for Heaven, though not the heaven with clouds, but God's heaven—you can watch television, even those wrestling films that I liked before loving God and that I don't like any more. But not now. God doesn't like violence and even if someone hits us, we mustn't complain. God likes it when someone hits us and we don't strike back, and whoever hits us becomes the devil and we become like Jesus, who is God, and allowed everyone in the world to hit him. And so I allow everyone to hit me, to be like Jesus, but without wanting to be Jesus, because wanting to be Jesus is a sin. We need to be like Jesus, without being Jesus, without wanting to be God, because there is only one God, who is three people. If we hit back at those who hit us, then we become like them, and we become like the devil too. Because hitting someone is like having sex: it feels good, and God doesn't like us feeling that relief, like getting rid of an itch that's bothering us, which is usually other people. So when we have sex, when we beat someone up, we get rid of that itch that was bothering us, the desire to feel relief, and then we enjoy life. And God doesn't like that. God likes it when we die, because then he can give us good things that he can't give us while we're alive. Because, when we die, God can be kind to us and God likes being kind. But if God is kind to us while we're alive, then we take advantage of that and stop loving God. We just enjoy the good things that are not Godly. We just want to have sex. We just want to hit back at the people who hit us, we want to spend our time enjoying football, opposing the government. We want God to be kind to us all the time. But God can only be kind to us when we die, because by then we've already felt a lot of that agony that God likes. God doesn't like it when we enjoy things that aren't Godly. God doesn't like it when we enjoy good things. While we're still alive, we must only like bad things.

But the sorts of bad things that we don't enjoy, not the bad things that the devil sends us, because those are good things, because the devil gives us those good things to make us stop loving God, which only brings us bad things, because we should be feeling agony so that God will continue to like us, let's not forget what happened to Adam who spent his time having sex with Eve instead of loving God. Not the devil, though. The devil gives us good things while we're alive and then, when we're dead, which is when we should be enjoying good things, he gives us bad things for all eternity. And that is truly horrible agony, because that suffering never stops, ever. We just long for relief and there never is any relief. And there's no use in trying to have sex with the pretty women in hell, because the women who are pretty are there to make us burn in hell. And if you want to have sex with them they bite and skewer you instead of having the kind of sex that is so good to have when you're alive, but which is bad because God doesn't like it. Another thing God doesn't like is when we make money, that's why I'll be poorer every day. I'll use my money only to buy food. But bad food, because God doesn't like us to eat tasty food. Because tasty food makes us stop loving God, because we enjoy food when it's tasty. Because food is like sex. It's like hitting someone we don't like. We get that sense of relief when we eat and stop being hungry. We have to eat things we don't enjoy, like the fatty bits in cheap cuts of meat, and as soon as we start feeling our hunger passing we must stop eating, so we won't feel any relief. Ah, yes! Money must also buy us clothes, because God doesn't want us to go naked. We must use clothes so we're not naked. God is against nakedness. We need clothes so we won't see the women naked and won't want to have sex with them. That's why the woman I'm going to marry will wear long dresses, so I never see her naked and think she's pretty. She has to wear dresses like the ones those horrible and hairy women use to hide their non-existent beauty. Because God doesn't like women to shave their legs, so they won't be like those women with golden stubble on their legs, to distract us, men, from loving God. They are there, hairless, but later will be skewering and roasting us in hell, which truly exists. My wife's clothes will be ugly. To please God, we must be ugly, too. My wife is pretty, with no hair on her legs, no varicose veins, and not fat, but I told her she has to become at least a little bit ugly. That way I won't want to have sex with her all the time, or love her too much. And when we want to make children I won't enjoy sex with her, because she'll be a little bit ugly, which is better. And so our children will also be born ugly, because they'll inherit whatever is ugly about us. I'm already ugly, thank God, and my wife will become ugly as soon as we get married, during the honeymoon, which we won't have because God doesn't like it, because honeymoons are only for having sex though I won't enjoy it because my wife will become ugly. Later, when my wife dies, she'll be able to become pretty again so I can have sex with her and won't have to have sex with those hairy women with varicose veins that God likes. And another thing: we have to mistreat women, that way they won't like us and it becomes easier for us not to like them and not to want to have sex, which God doesn't like. That's why we have to hassle our women, so they'll only love God instead of loving us, and so we'll only love God instead of loving them. So, as I was saying, with the money I'll make, which isn't much, just enough to be poor, and to become rich when I die, I will only buy bad clothes and bad food. The rest of my money I'm giving to God, because, when I die, God will pay me back twice the amount. And then I'll spend a lot of money, because money will be worthless and we'll be allowed to spend it. We'll be allowed to spend it on things that are of no use, but which we like. Because useless things are good, and the ones that are really useful, like God, are bad. But it's good for us to learn how to do things properly, so we can go to Eder, where everything is good, because there you are allowed to do even the bad things. Up there in Eder, we can earn lots of money that we don't need. But not now. Because now we do need money. Right now money is useful, but it isn't good to have any, otherwise we love our money too much and forget about loving God. When I die, I'll be allowed to eat good food. When my wife dies, she'll be pretty again. When I die, I'll eat manna, though I don't know what it tastes like, but it must be better than barbequed meat, which, before I loved God, I used to eat often with my work colleagues whenever there was a celebration. Now I won't ever like barbeques again. God doesn't like barbeques, because barbequed meat is tasty and people drink beer and ogle their female work colleagues. They stare at the tiny shorts. God likes long dresses over the hairy, varicose-veined legs of the women God likes. God likes us to eat bad meat, tough and fatty. God doesn't like it when we eat those top sirloin steaks, all bloody. It's because the blood is a reminder of the blood of Jesus, who is God. You can have meat that isn't bloody, meat that doesn't even look like it came from a cow. Blood is the problem. Blood makes things tastier because of that relief thing. Because we enjoy watching unpleasant people bleed, and we feel relief because it isn't us bleeding. God likes it when it's us bleeding. So we mustn't enjoy it when others bleed, because that makes them like Jesus and we become like the Romans and Jews who liked to see Jesus' blood, which was God's blood. And so everyone's blood becomes God's blood, except ours, because we must enjoy bleeding, so that the devil won't have any more blood to take when we die. But we mustn't enjoy cow's blood, because cows are almost like our neighbours. Cows are almost like women who also bleed every month, because God doesn't like women and made Eve bleed every month, for her to feel agony, which was good because she learned not to give Adam the apple and not to spend the entire day naked in Eder, with all her bits on display. God doesn't like things to be on display. And so it's all the same thing, thy neighbour's blood, the blood of naked women, cows' blood. Everyone must feel pain and bleed. And we mustn't enjoy watching our neighbour bleed, or women, because they bleed so we won't want to have sex with them and make a bloody and horrible mess. So we mustn't enjoy the blood in those top sirloins. Because cows are also God's children, but in a different way. God made the cows, although the cows don't know there is a God. They don't understand, don't think. To know that there is a God, we have to think, we have to wonder about whether the world exists, and the things in it, like cows and all those things that exist only because there is a God. Because if there were no God, there would be nothing, how could there be anything if God didn't exist? Who was going to make us think about God? Like me, who thinks about God, who knows there is a God, who loves God instead of loving women and cow steaks. When I think, I think only about God, because God doesn't want us to think too much about things that aren't Godly, like football isn't Godly. God wants us, humans, to think only so that we may know that God exists. We don't need to think a lot about other things because God wants us to be stupid, like donkeys.

But not like the donkey that God made to carry Mary, Our Lady, who isn't God because God is a man, but is the mother of Jesus, who is God. Donkeys, like cows, are stupid because they don't know there is a God. No animal knows there is a God. Only us, humans, who aren't stupid, but we mustn't want to be too smart and better than God. We, humans, must use our minds only to understand there is a God. We mustn't think about anything more than that, or else we start wondering whether there really is a God, and if there isn't, all the pain we have to enjoy has no reason, it's only suffering, and it won't end when we die, because if there is no God we won't be able to have sex in Eder, not even with the hairy women, and then it's all bad for no good reason,

if there is no God. Only us, humans, have that problem with thinking too much. We, humans, are the only rational animals that know there is a God. That's why all other animals exist to serve man. And man serves God. Man is God's animal.

So God can kill man whenever he wants, like man can also kill cows. Cows don't mind humans eating them. Since cows can't think, they don't know that humans are going to eat them. They don't have the problem with thinking. So all is good. So you can kill cows and eat them and it's not a problem and it's not even a problem to kill thy neighbour, who is human and needs to suffer so he can go to Eder. Cows don't suffer because they don't know there is a God, so they can just eat grass, in peace, without thinking about anything, just being, without knowing that we, humans, are going to catch them, bash them on their head to eat their meat. You just can't eat cows that are too bloody so it won't be a reminder of Christ's blood. If we eat bloodless cows, when we die we'll be born again and then we'll be able to eat bloody cows, which are tastier. Cows, when they die, are also born again so we can eat them when we die. And so they die and are born again, they die again and are born again, so we always have something to eat. Because we, humans, only die once and then we live forever, for eternity. We, humans, have two lives. One is bad and another is good. But if the first one is good, the second will be bad, and that makes it much worse, because the second one is longer than the first and it's better to live for longer having a good time than having a bad time. So that first life, which is the one we're in now, our real life, is the bad life, with hard stringy meat, with horrible hairy women who bleed every month. It's the life of suffering, the one we mustn't enjoy. And the other life, which is longer, is the one we'll have when we die, it's the good life, where you can even eat bloody top sirloin steaks, because when we die everything red becomes the blood of Jesus Christ, like wine, which is the blood of Jesus even in this life we have now, which is the bad life. That's why I no longer support Corinthians.

That Year in Rishikesh
Adriana Lisboa

I look at the world and I notice it's turning
—George Harrison

It happened when I was trying to play "While my guitar gently
weeps". Of the four, George was always my kind of Beatle. I feel
we could have been great friends, apart from that thing of him
being a Hare Krishna, which today sounds a bit too much and
I suspect would not be quite as fashionable. But it's easy to
understand why at the time the whole Indian mystic routine
might have been cool, it was new, it was different, it was an
alternative to everything that was there and in fact might still
be here but doesn't seem to bother anyone as much.

I admired him also for being a calm Beatle, with the quiet
demeanour of someone who has taken a few steps back, has
become a sort of spectator, while others croak and jump around
like hyperactive toads. John was the man for moments of rage.
Paul was the man to say good morning, sun. Ringo was the guy
who would come and show his support when I was I feeling
down, because in Ringo's company nothing could be taken very
seriously. And George was George, the quiet one – L'Angelo
Misterioso. He was asked on a television programme if, among
the four, he was the one who got the most girls, because girls like
quiet men like him, with an air of mystery about them. George
said no, the one who got the most girls among the four of them
was Paul.

It's a shame that George died so many years ago. Yes, it's a
shame about John, too, but there was something about George

dying of lung cancer, having survived throat cancer –they say he suffered horribly with the cancer that finally killed him, and that one day his doctor took his family (his, the doctor's) to visit him and they all started singing and making quite a racket and George, hardly able to breathe, asked them to please stop talking. And that the doctor made George autograph a guitar for his son. And George said I don't know if I can even sign my name, and the doctor spelled it out. Come on, you can do it. G E O R.

John came up against his instant karma as he left his home one day. There was nothing instant about George's karma, it was a karma operated by an eight-armed Chinese torturer, muttering the universal mantra in a strident and unpleasant voice, without a minute's pause, and smiling with fire in his eyes. But I think Hare Krishnas believe in reincarnation and it's fair that a person's existence and its aftermath should conform to the person's beliefs, so it's possible that George might come back in some sensational life form after going through that.

Although –let's be honest: what other life form could be more sensational after someone was born a Beatle and composed "While my guitar gently weeps"? Perhaps George will reincarnate as another type of Beatle in another planet or another dimension where cancer does not exist and, by implication, neither do oncologists or names spelled out for an autographed guitar. (Someone should release Mark Chapman and set him on the trail of that doctor.)

I was in my grandmother's bedroom. She was already at a stage of her illness in which she became easily irritated, she lived in a permanent state of confusion, sometimes she started a sentence and stopped halfway through. It was more or less six months before she died and some five years after she was diagnosed.

My grandmother was 82 years old. She didn't like being alone. She had lost a lot of weight and I was amazed by how thin her wrists and ankles were. Especially her ankles. Almost overnight she had withered, dried out like plums left too long in the refrigerator, her skin had turned into a surface resembling the fake leather handbag that my mother bought from a street vendor in the city centre, adorned with the letters MK, which I think are the initials of some fashion designer. And I looked at my grandmother and thought about George and about why people are forced to keep on living when there is clearly no point to it. When evil oncologists come to spell out your name so you can autograph their son's guitar. When someone no longer remembers what they did that morning and has difficulty recognising their only grandchild –me, in my grandmother's case. Her karma, too, was far from instant.

She did not like being alone, so when the girl who took care of her had some time off and my mother was not at home I'd go to her room. Curtains had to be permanently closed because she thought that someone in the building across the road was trying to spy on her, to spy on our family. And I explained that no one was trying to spy on us and my grandmother shook her head and said, I know what they did to Cristina. Cristina died. They killed her. I didn't know who Cristina was and she wouldn't say, not even when I asked. Sometimes she would start explaining and stop half way, though not suddenly, her voice would become more remote, like a train heading into the distance until it disappears behind a curve. Or she cried, a hushed cry, and I could tell only by the way her tear-sodden cheeks glistened, and I didn't know what to do. But almost immediately she'd forget her face was moist with tears, and she'd take my hand, would ask me to sit by her side, and would say: Gosh, how you've grown, Artur. The love I felt for her was like being harpooned, it was a tightness inside my chest, and I'd put my other hand over hers and say Gran, my name isn't Artur.

One of those days, I took my guitar and amplifier to her bedroom, into that muffled half-gloom, as if the air inside were denser than elsewhere. Not that it was bad. After a while it was strange, uncomfortable, I began to feel claustrophobic and tried to persuade her to go to the living room (sometimes she went; sometimes I turned on the television, but she couldn't pay attention for more than five minutes). At first it was fine, it was as if I were entering my grandmother's world, a world that was cooler and duskier and smelled like rose water. It was almost possible to think like she did, to feel like she did, to share that space of confusion behind her face, which would sometimes lose any trace of expression making her look uncannily like a mannequin. Except that mannequins in shops are in their twenties.

Gran. Would you mind if I play?

She looked at me, said huh?

Would you mind if I play? and I lifted the guitar.

But she didn't reply, she merely sighed and looked towards the window as if the window were not covered by a curtain and as if behind it there were some melancholy English landscape.

I took that to mean okay, I switched on the amplifier, turned the volume down. I started from the top with "While my guitar gently weeps", the riff that George played on the White Album (the guitar solo was by Eric Clapton, although his credit is not on the record), humming the tune and adding scraps of lyrics here and there.

My grandmother looked at me. I looked at her. I stopped playing, thinking that I might be making her uncomfortable. I thought about George dying and having to ask his doctor's family to please stop talking. But she just looked at me, saying nothing.

I carried on from where I had stopped. When I got to the part that says *I look at the world*, etc, she was smiling and shaking her head to the music. When I stopped she said, that's my favourite.

Your favourite?

I remember him playing that song for us, that year in Rishikesh.

Who is he?

You know, darling. George Harrison. George Harrison from the Beatles.

I was reminded of when my grandmother used to say she had been the girlfriend of Tancredo Neves. Very little of what she said, nowadays, could be taken seriously. I had the impression that everything was rolling around in her brain as if it were a large blender, and the gloop she processed (the smoothie, the milkshake) mixed past, present, dreams, imaginings, films, books, news, anything. She could have been the first woman to step on the moon, she could have lived in Paris or India, been a bus driver, a famous visual artist, a cleaner. The only things beyond her reach were those parts of her mind that disease had gnawed on. The rest was like items on a supermarket shelf, which you can help yourself to in no particular order– although paying for it at the till is quite another story. But the disease was strange, it seemed to preserve grand, old facts and rob my grandmother precisely of what she would find most useful. Or perhaps it was a way of anaesthetising her as, day after day, hour after hour, it dragged her away from life.

George Harrison played that song for you, Gran?

That year we spent in Rishikesh studying with His Holiness, she said.

She paused, rummaged around in her head.

His Holiness the Maharishi Mahesh Yogi. I remember he laughed a lot.

George Harrison laughed a lot?

His Holiness laughed a lot, she said, and laughed as well, and for a moment put her joined palms against her chest. I had never seen her do that before.

Can you play other songs? she asked.

Other Beatles songs?

She nodded. I played my entire repertoire, which was mostly songs by The Beatles plus "Band on the Run", which is still 25 percent by The Beatles. And then she asked me to help her get to the living room, an unusual request, and she sat in her favourite armchair, she hadn't forgotten which one it was even though she sometimes couldn't remember if she liked figs and bananas or not. A few minutes later she was asleep.

I went back to my room feeling somewhat confused, with a mix of religious dread and fascination about my grandmother. I checked up on the story and found that, indeed, Rishikesh was the name of that Indian city where the Maharishi Mahesh Yogi had his ashram, and where the Beatles went in the sixties and where they composed many of their songs. It was incredible that my grandmother could associate the song I played with all of that. And that she remembered the song, and that it was by George, and all the rest. And that, on top of it all, she should insert herself in the story.

My mother arrived from work shortly after, carrying over-bromated bread and threatening envelopes bearing bank logos.

She left everything on the kitchen counter, asked how my grandmother was.

In the living room, having a nap, I said. Mum, you won't believe the story she told me.

I need a shower. And something for my headache. Tell me later –and in a continuous, fluid gesture she went into her room, dropped the handbag on the bed making the fake Italian designer's initials tinkle, picked up some clothes that were on the floor and made her way to the bathroom. I heard the shower running, and the water, tired and chlorinated, assuming the unenviable task of washing my mother's day away, off her body, her soul. She would also be applying products with special smells and packaging that made them look more expensive than they were.

My grandmother appeared in the corridor, loose hair escaping from her bun, shuffling her feet in the furry slippers that never quite fit. She walked past me, went to her room, opened the wardrobe.

Come here, lad, she called in her feeble voice.

I went to the door.

I need to get something from up there. Behind those boxes.

I climbed on a chair to reach what she wanted. I shifted boxes in various shapes and sizes, none of which had an identifiable purpose, I pulled out fabric bags that smelled of mildew. Until I found a soapbox and she said, that's it, give it to me. My grandmother's hands were stretched out and slightly tremulous –they were almost always tremulous, there was nothing particularly solemn about that moment. I would have displayed some solemnity if I'd know she was about to rummage inside the box, calmly and with bony fingers, sitting like a dwarf on her bed's yellow quilt, and pull out a photograph of her with George Harrison.

She handed me the photograph and said, Rishikesh. She mumbled a few things about His Holiness and also about Cynthia Lennon. George and my grandmother were wearing white tunics, with short hair and saffron coloured flower garlands. My grandmother had a little red spot between her eyebrows. She could have been George's older sister.

We spent the afternoon of the following day playing and singing, sharing stories –some true, others not, what did it matter?—about The Beatles. We spent many other afternoons doing that. She told me what songs she wanted me to learn, and I learned them.

Until one day, with no warning and no drama, my grandmother died. I don't know if she remembered my name or if I was only that lad who played her favourite songs on the guitar, some avatar of the music by the quartet from Liverpool that had come her way as if by miracle. A gift sent by the Maharishi from a world beyond? My grandmother no longer needed to find logic in things, or even to create a logic for things that apparently didn't have one. The world was one big trip, Lucy in the sky with diamonds.

After she died, we went to sort out her wardrobe. The cotton clothes, the furry slippers that never quite fit her. The jumble of bags and boxes. My mother cried, and I hugged her, and later, when there was no one else around, I cried too. I kept the soapbox full of unidentified treasures. Things that had made sense to my grandmother, things that had made her life gentler, provided the comfort of accumulation when she had innocently believed it would last forever –like most of us do, death being something that happens to other people.

In the soapbox was her employment record card, letters with

handwriting from a time when people studied handwriting under the guidance of nuns and priests, an empty perfume jar. And some photographs: apart from the Rishikesh relic, all seemed to be family or school souvenirs, girls vaguely similar to characters in old films. I looked through the photographs to find other Beatles pictures, there were none.

One of them, however, caught my eye. My grandmother was very young. How long ago had that scene been photographed? She was holding hands with a man. It was sunny and both were squinting and even with the photograph being old and faded there could be no doubt: it was Tancredo Neves. I looked out of her bedroom window, sitting on her bed with its yellow quilt. Pigeons flew outside beyond the open curtains, in a world that was strangely calm, strangely ordinary.

Flipping at Flip
or Remembrance of Crumbs Past
Reinaldo Moraes

—Are you going to see Crumb?

I've been asked some ten times already, and that's just today. It's the same question that thousands of people crowded into this 18th century town ask each other during the 2010 edition of the Festa Literária Internacional de Paraty, the now popular Flip, which this year pays homage to a sociologist from Pernambuco, Gilberto Freyre. I came as a guest author and also, of course, to hear the chatter of a small group of fiction writers appearing alongside a larger gang of thinkers in the fields of culture, society and politics, with a few comic-book artists thrown into the mix. Rumour had it that even an American rock-star-turned-poet would be here, but at the very last minute the darling man decided "to send Lima" in his place. "Fuck those jungle monkey schmucks!" he must have said outside his Brooklyn home, before deciding not to travel to Brazil. ("To send Lima", for those who don't know, is old-fashioned musicians' slang for slipping away from the band and not showing up for a gig.)

The opening lecture of the *eveiinto*, as we in São Paulo call an event, was proffered by a politician with an academic background who was never regarded as a great stylist of the Portuguese language, despite being a captivating speaker ("gives good lip", as Homem-Legenda, the character by cartoonist Adão Iturrusgarai would put it), an essential attribute in anyone who loves audiences and wants to be president – like he was, twice.

"Who wants to hear Fernando Henrique Cardoso talking about Gilberto Freyre? Has the Festa sold out to the toucans [social democrats]?" asked Marcelino Freire, the São Paulo-based short-story author from Pernambuco, throwing a stone at Flip's glass windows in an interview with *Folha de S. Paulo*. It was only one of the many grievances expressed by a handful of writers peeved at Flip 2010's apparent sucking up to the establishment. Many people from São Paulo's "literary quarter" (that is, those who drink at Mercearia São Pedro, in the heights of Vila Madalena) whined because fiction writers (most of whom, including myself, were attending Flip for the second time) were outnumbered and outsmarted by academics.

Yes, yes, yes, I've been to Flip twice, with first class hotel and all the niceties, for me and my wife (Marta García, an editor at Companhia das Letras), though no payment except a bottle of Maria Izabel cachaça (very good), an S sized t-shirt (I'm 1.92 m, and use XL) and a lovely recycled paper notebook, far from the mythical Moleskine used by 9 out of 10 snobbish writers the world over.

My role at Flip is to be part of a panel that includes two other writers of fiction, that is, of stories that never happened recounted with some narrative skill. My fellow panellists are Ronaldo Correia de Brito, a Recife-based writer from Ceará who sets his pared down tales in the northeastern backlands, and São Paulo's Beatriz Bracher, a writer connected to her innermost femininity, on which she offers some interesting perspectives. According to Flip's official catalogue, I have just written "an instant classic of sardonic humour". None of us has anything in common with any of the others, which seems to be our panel's guiding principle.

At Flip, the intellectual displays, often amounting to narcissistic verbal incontinency, are called *mesas*, or round tables, and take place in the Authors' Marquee, an inflatable rubber and aluminium pavilion built near the banks of the Perequê river, not far from the sea. But it is at the tables in bars, often in the open air, that the conversation flows freely, chasing thoughts steeped in beer and in the fortified local cachaça, which warms the soul but tortures the head the following morning.

Like I said, this is the second time I've been a guest at Flip, for reasons that are beyond my comprehension. They must think I look good in photographs, or who knows, they might like the early-morning-drunk tone of my voice. The first time was in 2006, when I shared the stage with André Santanna and Lourenço Mutarelli, great guys with whom I also have very little in common, in literary terms. Not that it matters. For me, these are opportunities to see faraway friends, drink a lot of cachaça, enjoy glorious fish stews and eat lots of seafood, courtesy of whoever happens to be paying. That year, a mega-bank and the state of Rio de Janeiro were the main sponsors among dozens of other companies. I don't care who is providing the largesse, as long as the fish is served in a decent prawn sauce and the cachaça is Maria Izabel, the best in Paraty.

If truth be told, I've been to almost all previous editions of the *Festa Literária*, from the first one –the best—in 2003, with almost no policemen or private security guards on the streets, and a pleasant *laissez-faire* atmosphere that gave the tri-centenarian Paraty the feeling of a tropical Amsterdam. Maurice of Nassau would have had fun here, with so much cachaça and so many good-looking chicks running loose in the streets. Today, when it is much bigger and richer, the literary happening is more thoroughly policed and more tightly controlled, which makes it difficult for an artist to light up a spliff or relieve his bladder in a well-shaded corner.

(Okay, pissing in the street is not on, but where is the cleaner alternative for a drunkard sailing through the town's deserted night? Flip has chemical toilets, but they're available only near the Festa's marquees, and they're not open through the night. Apart from that, there are no public urinals or shit-houses other than those in restaurants and bars, and they are not always open to the public. The thing to do, then, is to throw caution to the wind, look up at the moon and go for it. If dogs do it on the streets all the time, why not a more evolved being who has just spent a small fortune on the taxes included in the price of his ice-cold beer?)

I missed the Festa's opening, a lecture on Gilberto Freyre by Big Fernando H.C., followed by a show with Edu Lobo and a constellation of "emerging talents in Brazilian Popular Music", even though I had a badge that got me into all the events. The fact is that I can't stand being lectured by people with microphones. As ever, I preferred the spontaneous prose of life on the streets, much more stimulating for the mind than for the liver. And if there is something good about Paraty it is its streets, which are more like canals paved with enormous cobblestones so far away from each other that they test pedestrians' skills. At least no one has to fight over space with motorised vehicles, which are not allowed in the city centre.

But it's tricky to jump from one cobblestone to the next when your psychomotor system is drenched in sugarcane spirits. And if the cobbles happen to be wet with rain –hello orthopaedist! There should be a sign in bars saying: "Don't drink and walk". The ideal solution would be litter chairs, moved around by two strong youths hoping to stay in shape by carrying drunks, lazy people and wheelchair users up and down the streets of Paraty, and perhaps even earning some tips for their efforts. Gilberto Freyre, a declared enthusiast of Brazil's colonial habits, including slavery, would surely have applauded the idea.

On Wednesday, when I arrived for Flip's opening sessions, there was a lot of chatter about whether it was appropriate to have an old and still quite influential politician delivering the *eveiinto*'s inaugural lecture in the middle of an election year. Besides creating more attention for the PSDB, Fernando Henrique's party, it seemed uncharacteristic of Flip. Writer Márcia Denser, who was at Flip some years ago when she appeared in a documentary by Bruno Barreto, let rip in one of her postings on her website *Congresso em Foco*: "Flip does not celebrate Literature, or writers, and much less Brazilian authors, but only the publishing market, the merchandising of nation-less literature. In other words, barbarity."

*

In any case, the question remains: what has that got to do with literature? The answer, very typical of "toucans" educated at the University of São Paulo, could well be: is there anything that hasn't got to do with literature? Everything can fit into that generous sack-full of cats. Literature is like the churches of old, which kept their doors open and welcomed all sorts of people, from the mighty and prosperous figures to the drunk, the wretched, the mad and the murderers – without forgetting the packs of stray dogs that came in to sniff the incense and bite the young ladies' shins.

As soon as I arrived in Paraty I was marched over to the official welcome lunch in the courtyard of Pousada da Marquesa, one of the poshest in town, along with other guest authors, organisers, sponsors, journalists and the usual party-crashers. As I stood in the queue for the prawn *bobó*, I observed the heir to the Brazilian throne, Dom João de Orléans e Bragança, good looking and with impeccably styled hair, dressed to the tees with casual wear from Richards, always with the hint of a smile on his noble lips, as if ready to pronounce some gallantry in tune with these democratic times. He has a lovely house here, by the seaside, where I have had lunch in the past. Dom João must be the biggest local landlord, the beneficiary of the old tax that the nobility was once allowed to levy from tenants living on their property. That's if Brazil's "Citizen's Constitution" of 1988 did not abolish the *enfiteuse*, that strange French name for such a tax. I imagine that, in France, the French Revolution abolished that institution in 1789. In Brazil, however, such privileges tend to have a longer life.

I asked myself if Gilberto Freyre, were he alive, would have the humility to queue alongside writers who are better known around the world than him, like Salman Rushdie. (That's right, folks, I saw Salmon queuing for prawn. I was holding a knife in my hand. If Khomeini's *fatwa* were still in place, I could have claimed the millions of dollars as a reward for slitting his throat right there. Since I have never been in jail before, I'd be out in six months, at most, as free as a taxi, like that journalist who shot his girlfriend ten years ago out of jealousy.)

It's true that, despite my reservations, Gilberto Freyre – "the Proust of Brazilian sociology", as his fellow sociologist Gilberto

Vasconcellos calls him—has something to do with literature, since he is considered a fine prose writer who took an interest in the daily activities of people in the colonial period, including sex, food, marriage, work, slave labour –the raw material for historians, sociologists, writers and other liars.

More than once I have immersed myself in the hundreds of pages of *The Masters and the Slaves* without ever finishing the book. I confess I find his prose pretentious, too showy and class-oriented, though the many anecdotes and colourful stories he tells make it entertaining. By contrast, Machado de Assis and Father Vieira, though not quite Beatniks, don't sound pretentious at all. Anyway, let them fight it out.

Besides, who am I to speak well or ill about Gilberto Freyre, that acknowledged admirer of dictatorships (Vargas, Brazil's military dictatorship, and Portugal's Salazar), declared anti-Semite and racist, if I'm not mistaken, who became a darling of the elites by saying, in the 1930s, that Brazilian slaves were well treated and might even be considered co-colonisers, alongside their Portuguese masters who, however, always preferred to remain on the right side of the whip. The point is that everyone knows about that now –even I know— because thanks to Flip these stories have been appearing in all the newspaper supplements for weeks.

Despite his ancestral racism, Freyre became a cheerleader for the miscegenation that shaped the Brazilian people, a phenomenon embodied in the genes of the pretty local girl I met here, twenty-something, one foot in an Indian village and the other hovering somewhere between Portuguese caravels and the African slave galleys. She works at a bar on Praça da Matriz where I went for a drink on Flip's opening night with my friend Marechal, full-time journalist and Carioca, whose

godfather was none other than Nelson do Cavaquinho.
Marechal also noticed the little Indian girl, as old timers among
the New Wavers (and here I include myself –even if I have no
Lambretta, don't own ankle boots, don't wear my shirt collar up
and don't slick my hair back) would have described her.
Everyone noticed the local beauty.

I have known Marechal for 5 or 6 years, and have only seem
him 5 or 6 times, always at Flip, enough to establish the sort of
intimacy one might have with a classmate from nursery school,
despite the 20 odd years by which I predate him.

The eugenically miscegenated waitress –Angélica was her
perfect name—served us beer and a cachaça that was not Maria
Izabel. "It's one of Maria Izabel's cousins," she had told us with
a remarkable sense of humour. We quaffed the alcoholic cousin
while the fancier audiences packed the Authors' Marquee,
a true Tent of Intellectual Miracles, where FHC discoursed
on the sociologist from Pernambuco, without sparing him
a few politically correct blows, or so I was told, basically for
being a racist, an anti-Semite and an elitist. My wife, Marta,
who is afflicted by the chronic student syndrome, and could not
resist being at the opening lecture, told me about the roaring
success of the prince of Brazilian sociologists. "He's great!",
she said when I met her later that night. But not as great as that
girl from the bar, I said to myself in cautious silence.

That first night I decided to give up the partying relatively
early, shortly after 2 a.m., since the following day I would be on
stage at 3 p.m., and it is always advisable to be awake when
facing an audience. With great difficulty I managed to negotiate
the town centre's cobblestones and find my way to the flat road
on the riverside leading to various hotels, mine included.Early
in the morning, in the breakfast room, as I sipped some coffee in

an attempt to coax some of my neurons into facing the day ahead, someone else asked:

—Are you going to see Crumb?

—Yes, I'm going to see crumbs— I replied, flicking some sweetcorn-cake crumbs off my lap. In fact, I intended to attend every *mesa*, despite having already missed FHC's opening lecture.

Crumb, Crumb, Crumb. That's all anyone talks about in this town. Besides meaning "a very small piece broken from a baked item", crumb also means, according to the Web's *Free Dictionary*, "a contemptible, untrustworthy, or loathsome person". Someone despicable, then. With Lou Reed's last-minute cancellation, Mr Despicable became Flip's great attraction, and everyone wants to see him live, as if that would cure people of some chronic illness, like asthma or psoriasis.

The creator of comic books such as *Fritz the Cat* and *Mr. Natural* ("Keep on trucking," was the bearded baldy's motto) that I read in the 1970s, Crumb had remained hidden somewhere, averse to running into journalists and photographers, to whom he gave the bird when snapped on the street. And people loved that. Apparently, to be told by a celebrity to stick a finger up there where the sun doesn't shine is the cause of great jubilation around here. I read in the papers that his friend and fellow cartoonist Gilbert Shelton, creator of *The Freak Brothers*, had been less aggressive but no less evasive. I used to like *The Freak Brothers*, which I could find at the bookstore in Congonhas airport, alongside Crumb's titles, back in the days when we used to drive out there with our girlfriends to drink coffee and watch airplanes take off and land – an incomprehensible outing for a Carioca, for instance, who would never consider going to Santos Dumont airport to get a caffeine shot and browse foreign magazines at the local bookshop, surrounded by the roar of Constellation and Elektra aircraft owned by the long-defunct Vasp, Varig or Cruzeiro do Sul.

Freewhelin' Jack, Shelton's lean Freak brother, was my favourite. Along with Charlie Brown and Mafalda he was among my post-adolescent comic-book heroes. During my first European trip, in 1975, I saw an adaptation of *Fritz the Cat* in London. I remember vaguely that the cat called Fritz spent a lot of time screwing girls on the street and doing all sorts of mad stuff. I didn't like the film much, and apparently Crumb himself hated it. It is well known that it was his wife, Aline, who sold the rights to the film's director, Ralph Bakshi, behind Crumb's back. Instead of giving his wife a hard time about it, Crumb killed Fritz in his next comic strip, thus ending the delinquent cat's career.

In any case, they were all there, in the same town as me: Crumb, Aline (who is also an illustrator), Shelton and his wife, Lora Fountain, who became the trio's agent. Yet I was unable to get too excited by their physical proximity. I found the presence of Angélica, the waitress from the bar on the square, much more stimulating. Knowing she was in the area, offering beer, cachaça and dazzling smiles to her customers and admirers, meant that I had no eyes for anyone else in Paraty –Crumb, Shelton and FHC included.

And so my time arrived to make an appearance in the Shrine, by which I mean the Authors' Marquee. While I awaited the call to sacrifice in my hotel room, I heard someone speaking in a northeastern accent. Marta, who was coming through the door, whispered: "It's your event colleague, Ronaldo Brito, he's on his bedroom balcony, reading his text out loud."

"What text?" I asked. Marta did not know either, but soon I would find out from Ronaldo –who last year made 200 grand by bagging the São Paulo Prize with his novel *Galiléia* (whoa, envy!)—that he was rehearsing his reading of a passage from a short story for our event. He'd been rehearsing for at least four hours, he confessed, somewhat insecurely. In fact, when he is called upon to read his work in public, the celebrated writer from Crato spends many days rehearsing the text he will "perform". A theatre man, as he claims to be, besides being a novelist and medic, Ronaldo will go as far as hiring a theatre director to help with his performance. Yet, as I was able to verify, my colleague's performance merely consists of reading his text, seated like everyone else, with the occasional stutter. So much rehearsing for that? I concluded that he rehearses because he likes rehearsing, and that's that.

In the Green Room, located in a small tent behind the massive Authors' Marquee, we meet with Beatriz Bracher and make small talk, sipping cachaça and, in my case, lots of water to fend off last night's hangover. When I was back in São Paulo I had read some short stories from Ronaldo's book, *Faca*, and also from Bia Bracher's latest book, *Meu amor*. I thought it was my duty to know something about my fellow panelists. I discovered they write well, obviously, otherwise they wouldn't be there. Each had a distinctive "voice", to use the common expression. I thought of complimenting them both –"Beautiful narrative voices!"—but, partly because of the hangover and partly because of stage-fright, I couldn't muster the will to flatter anyone. Since no one flattered me, we were all even, and so we went on stage beneath the intense spotlights.

If there is something that has little to do with literature it is spotlights. Besides, you can't do literature on stage, in front of an audience. At a jazz, rock or Brazilian music festival, for instance, musicians get on stage and make music for us to hear. The same occurs with dance and theatre. You can even say the same about sex, as proven every day by the live sex shows all over the world. But it doesn't work with literature. How can you do literature in front of others? Only if you are an oral storyteller, or if you are replicating my friend Mário Prata's sponsored web experiment of 10 years ago. Pratinha would stay at home, and at an agreed time would start working on a police comedy which he wrote on-line and in front of a web-cam. From their own homes, web browsers could follow the writer in real time on their screens. They could make plot suggestions, which Prata would incorporate if possible. There were some 14,000 people linking up to him and his writing every day, over six months. A feat that even Paulo Coelho would be proud of. The final result – a novel called *The Angels of Badaró* – was published successfully by Objetiva, and was even reviewed by France's *Libération*. A great accomplishment, for sure.

Putting aside that extreme case of literary exhibitionism – which, to the best of my knowledge, was never repeated—the most that a writer can do in front of an audience is read his texts, which is what Bracher, Brito and I did. Each one of us read a short passage from our most recent books, and earned modest applause from those audience members who were still awake after our readings. Half way through this salon, however, one of the leather straps holding up my seat bottom snapped beneath me. The chair collapsed and I ended up on the floor just as Bia was starting to read, after spending some time explaining the passage she was about to read.

I had to get up and wait for a new chair, amid laughter and even a small wave of applause. I'm not sure that my unexpected performance can be classed under "literature", but it earned me, the following day, a photograph in the *Folha de S. Paulo,* looking unsteady on the broken chair. It won't be this sort of performance that earns me the Nobel, although after being applauded for falling off a chair I'm beginning to think anything is possible.

From then on, our panel went smoothly. Each one of us explained, for the umpteenth time, that authors are authors and characters are characters, and that the texts should speak for themselves, without the help of explanations from their authors at literary meetings –despite the fact that we were there doing just that. Nudged by the chairwoman, the enthusiastic and tactful professor of literature Cristiane Costa, we discussed a few trivialities about our "creative process". I doubt that Shakespeare or Cervantes were ever compelled to discuss their creative processes with a paying audience. Especially Cervantes, who seems to have developed his in a prison in 16th century Seville while writing part of *Don Quixote.*

At the end, the three of us were given an earnest round of applause before we were moved on to another marquee, on the other side of the river, where we spent some time signing copies of our books and posing for pictures and putting our arms around readers who had been charitable enough to dig into their pockets and buy our books. It was the moment when our "art" became merchandise. *Ars gratia accountis,* as the Latin saying goes. Or, as the writer Marcelo Mirisola said about Flip in an interview: "Everyone wins there! From the street vendors to the hotel owners, and even the publishers. But our writers go there to drink cachaça. Brazilian writers are so tacky!"

It was more or less how I felt at the Autograph Marquee: a tacky cachaça-drinker signing books. And guess what? Crumb did not show up to ask for my autograph. But many of my friends and acquaintances kept asking the same question, which was becoming a sort of mantra: "Are you going to see Crumb?"

To see or not to see Crumb? That is the question. The same one that was put to me again that night, at the party for Penguin Books, represented in Brazil by Companhia das Letras. A big celebration, with samba by Banda Glória, and lots of caipirinhas and lovely ladies –beginning with mine, of course. While the singer belted out some sambas by Paulinho da Viola, my friend Arnaldo Bloch introduced me to young Tatiana Salem Levy, a Portuguese-Brazilian writer of Turkish-Jewish ancestry. Arnaldo, already with a couple of caipirinhas inside him, blurted out: "Tatiana, this is Reinaldo Moraes, the author of that masterpiece, 'The Devil to Pay up the Back Passage'."

The caipirinhas I had imbibed myself prevented me from feeling any embarrassment. Tatiana laughed heartily, because that is what clever women do to defuse the vulgarity to which they are occasionally exposed. A dainty brunette, of the kind that a cheap charmer would call tasty, the Turco-Jewish-Brazilo-Portuguese writer (she was born in Lisbon) had also won 200 big ones with the São Paulo Literature Prize, like Ronaldo Correia de Brito, but in the First Novel category, with *A Chave da Casa*. She did not only discover the Keys to the House, but the keys to the coffers. Bless her!, as my grandmother might say.

After the usual greetings, Tatiana started asking me a whole range of somewhat personal questions. "Married? Children? How many? Do you make your living by writing? Where in São Paulo do you live? Why did you switch publishers? What are you writing now?" The only thing she didn't ask was whether my prostate was in its usual place, and how many times a month I performed my spousal duties. As a result, within five minutes it felt like we were old friends, a development that my wife's vigilant gaze seemed not quite to approve of.

Amid our small talk, I remembered having read somewhere that Tatiana was involved last year with an overhyped and much older Portuguese writer, whose name I could not remember. No, I said to myself, it cannot be Eça de Queiroz. Or Ramalho Ortigão. (Only now was I able to Google it and dispel the mystery: Tatiana's elderly Portuguese man-of-love was Miguel Sousa Tavares, author of *Rua das Flores* and *Equador*, celebrated novels that, I suspect, I will never read in this incarnation, out of sloth, mostly, since they are veritable doorstops.)

Tatiana continued her line of interrogation, demanding to know how I write my books, how long it takes me to produce a novel, that sort of thing. Faced by a pair of beautiful and attentive dark-brown eyes, I revealed without hesitation my well kept secret: "I sit down and I write," I whispered to her. And I added: "Hours on end, day and night, every bloody day, for years –five years, with my latest book, *Pornopopéia*."

With a slight air of superiority, mademoiselle Salem Levy told me that her prize-winning book took much less than that, and that she writes only in the mornings, no more than two hours. "And then?", I wanted to know, becoming as nosy as her. "Then? Well, then I do whatever I feel like," she replied. I wondered privately what the young lady feels like doing after writing, but couldn't ask, because my wife Marta pushed me onto the dance floor, and ended our conversation.

Up to that point I had missed all the day's events, except my own, obviously. I had missed some important people, like Moacyr Scliar, Patrícia Melo and an American author of dense psycho-thrillers called Lionel Shriver. Arnaldo Bloch pointed Lionel out to me at the same party. I realised, with some surprise, that Mr Lionel was, in fact, a slender blonde woman in her fifties wearing high-heeled shoes. Nice heels, I thought. I imagined myself having an affair with her, if only to be able to write a torrid account called "In bed with Lionel". But I went nowhere near her. I simply threw back a few more caipirinhas, all the better for being free, and danced a few sambas with my wife before we took off in the early hours, rocking over Paraty's blessed cobblestones.

The next day, at breakfast, some elegant ladies in their sixties came to congratulate me for my performance the day before. One of them offered this jewel: "Congratulations on your irreverence." I thanked them, thinking: *cazzo*, I've gotten into all sorts of trouble for my loose-mouthed irreverence, but I had never been congratulated for it. By an old auntie with a *foulard* around her neck, highlights in her hair and varnished nails. The world definitely changed while I slept. The lady and her friends told me they hadn't missed a single Flip since 2003, and that they had already booked their hotel rooms for 2011. Long may they live, I thought, as I said goodbye with the best smile I could summon at that time.

I read the day's programme as I scooped papaya with a spoon. There were panels with *gringos* I had never heard of. Who was William Boyd? Who was A.B. Yehoshua? And Azar Nafisi? And there was Salman Rushie, who I haven't yet read, not even his infamous *The Botanic Verses*. I had seen him before in Paraty, the first time he came to Flip. Not to mention that I'd spotted him at the welcome lunch two days earlier. I told myself that I would go to see Salman Rushdie at seven thirty in the evening. But did I go? Of course not. At 7.30 p.m. there I was again with Marechal at the bar on the square, al fresco, wetting my lips with Maria Izabel's cousin, served by the hands of "my" fairy Indian princess with honeyed lips: Angélica.

At 10 p.m., as I considered asking for her hand in marriage, I realised that Angélica was no longer to be seen. With some difficulty I realised that I was no longer in the same bar. I had bar-hopped without realising it. It must have been some form of teleportation. Or perhaps a circumspect alcohol-fuelled amnesia, which does not stop me from remembering now that people kept asking, every twenty minute or so:

—Are you going to see Crumb tomorrow?

Yes, of course, I will see Crumb tomorrow, I have to see Crumb tomorrow, I shall see Crumb tomorrow, without a doubt I will see Crumb tomorrow.

The following day, Saturday, shrouded in the cruellest of cumulative hangovers, I gave in to a zen, aspirin-induced inertia and locked myself up in the hotel. Determined to shake me out of my lamentable state of hepatic exhaustion, my Marta pulled me out of bed at 2.30 p.m. and demanded that I join her at the inescapable Authors' Marquee. The dear wanted me to go along to the reading, by four Brazilian poets, of the fifty-odd poems in Carlos Drummond de Andrade's earliest book, *Alguma Poesia*, first published, if I'm not mistaken, in the 1930s. A shower and a few coffees later, there I was in the Tent of Miracles to see Ferreira Gullar, Antonio Cícero, Eucanaá Ferraz and Chacal, reading, one by one, Drummond's poems. I did not regret going, and not only because of Drummond, but because I am a friend and admirer of Chacal, whose best book, *Quampérius*, a mixture of marginal poetry and prose and pure adolescent mischief, had a big impact on me when I read it for the first time in 1976.

Five minutes into the reading, I was off to the land of nod. I had been transported to the realm of sleep, even in the presence of the slightly terrifying figure of Ferreira Gullar, a poet that, according to Nelson Rodrigues, looked like his own aunt. And that was in the '60s. Today, at 80, brave Gullar looks more like his own great grandmother. With or without Gullar, with or without Chacal, with or without Drummond, I made myself comfortable in the seat and drifted into the arms of Morpheus and of poetry, in that order, and enjoyed a lovely cat nap to the sound of the beautiful verses by the poet from Itabira. *In the methylene-blue sky, the ironic and diuretic moon looks like a dining-room print...*

Before I embarked on my forty winks, however, I had taken the precaution of asking my diligent wife to elbow me if I started to snore. I probably didn't, since I don't remember being elbowed. I didn't even have enough energy to snore. We left the Marquee, and I stumbled back to the hotel and fell into bed. I think I dreamed about a tempest of paper crumbs. I woke up feeling rested but with the clear sense of having missed something important, an appointment or a meeting. I only realised what it was when someone on the street asked me:
—Hey, did you see Crumb?

That's right, Crumb. I looked at the time on my mobile phone: 21:40. The event with Crumb and Shelton had finished only minutes earlier. In the end, I had failed to see the great Mr Despicable, the supreme cheese, the mighty Crumb. I shuddered down to my innermost ontological being: what would my life be like from now on, having missed my single chance to see Crumb?

Take it easy, I told myself, searching for consolation. It was Saturday night, and a lot of water had yet to flow beneath the bridge that links the old city centre to the Authors' Marquee, along with plastic bottles, supermarket bags and beer cans. Walking around the town centre I realised that, besides having missed Crumb, I had lost my favourite Flip drinking partner, the glorious Marechal, and even the waitress with the lips like honey and cachaça, who was no longer serving at the bar on the plaza. But I ran into other friends who had just seen Crumb and Shelton and had found the whole thing a mighty bore. It appears that the duo had made a display of its first-world tedium in front of an audience of amazed little monkeys. Shelton, acting out the part of his Freewheelin' Jack, seemed high as a kite and might not have been able to tell what country he was in, or why. While Crumb, the long-awaited for presence, barely let out monosyllables every now and then.

Marta –who had gone to see the pair and had been disappointed— told me: "It was unbelievably boring. At one point Crumb said: 'I don't know why you are here to see me go through this'."

By "go through this" he meant being subjected to the uncomfortable scrutiny of thousands of spectators, people in search of immediate entertainment and direct contact with global celebrities. And, to make matters worse, in the Third World. The audience expected Crumb to be an old uncle full of bizarre and funny stories. But the crazy uncle was not willing to offer any entertainment –or not to us, at least.

—You know what?—I said to Marta. –Fuck Crumb.

My adorable consort agreed and the two of us had dinner at a very reasonable bar offering a delicious shredded cod salad, which I wolfed down with the help of a bottle of Portuguese vinho verde, because man cannot live on fish alone. I was ready to end the day after the sweet Angel Hair we had for dessert, but Marta, after the Crumb fiasco, was eager for some dance-floor action. Women always want to dance. Women, to say the truth, always want something, as my friend Mario Bortolotto, so knowledgeable about the female soul, would say.

With no desire to party, I went along with my wife to the most promising of parties, thrown by a big publisher, I forget which one. Perhaps Record. There was a long queue at the door. Many of the people queuing had seen Crumb and were now taking great pleasure in trashing him and Shelton. I was in no mood to dance, drink standing up, or listen to people badmouthing Crumb, whom I hadn't even seen with these two eyes of mine that had once devoured his crazy comics. I suggested a strategic retreat. To my delight, and after seeing how packed the party was, the missus agreed. Once back in our private alcove, I repaid her solidarity as best I could, if you'll forgive me for saying so. It was the best night I spent in Paraty, even having missed Crumb and having lost the honey-lipped beauty and my friend Marechal. Love is strong.

The following morning, Sunday, the last day of Flip, besides one more mesa about Gilberto Freyre involving sociologists, anthropologists and historians (one specimen of each), and another about some obscure academic topic featuring some celebrated egg-heads, there was one that truly interested me: a conversation between women writers (wow!), featuring a Cuban blogger, Wendy Guerra, and a young novelist, Carola Saavedra, chaired by João Paulo Cuenca, author of *O Dia Mastroianni*, an excellent and somewhat mischievous novel that has God as one of its characters.

Carola was going to talk about her latest book, *Flores Azuis* – I read that one and liked it—which has an intriguing plot: a man, separated from his wife, moves into an apartment, and starts getting letters from a woman to her ex-husband, who happened to live there before. The new tenant reads the letters and is immediately drawn into the intimate recesses of the feminine soul (call Bortolotto!). The experience has a profoundly transformative effect on his life. Carola writes very well, and on top of that seems to be very charming, even though I've only ever actually seen her in an interview on the web.

I read in the press that the petite and well-read Wendy Guerra is a powerful voice of dissent and opposition to the Cuban dictatorship, always being boycotted by the Cuban government, which does not allow her books to be published on Castro's Fantasy Island. I found a website with nude photographs of the little lady, but since I fancy myself a bit of a gentleman, I won't reveal the address here. I don't know what led this Cuban girl to pose naked (perhaps she wanted to give old Fidel a heart attack), but I can guarantee that the result is a sight for the sore eyes of idle cybernauts of any ideological colour.

I needn't say that I missed that event, and all the others, except the day's (and the festival's) final one, in which some of the (few) Brazilian and foreign fiction writers at Flip would read passages from their favourite books. It is a Flip tradition that I had not witnessed until then, for the simple reason that I find literary salons powerfully tedious, when not downright soporific, as demonstrated by the previous day's Drummond session. But it so happens that I was one of the authors chosen to be a writer-reader, and there was no getting out of it. And so I went back to the Authors' Marquee.

Once again in the Green Room, behind the large tent, and waiting to go on stage, I found myself surrounded by a bunch of gringos I had never heard of before that Flip, apart from William

Kennedy, author of *Ironweed*, which became a lovely film, sad as hell, directed by Héctor Babenco. Conducting the event, beginning with the order in which the six chosen authors walked onto the stage, was Liz Calder, one of the Festa's founders. Also the co-founder of Bloomsbury, the British publisher of J.K. Rowling and her series of books starring one Harry Potter, Madame Calder retains the same jovial and cool air she had when I first met her in 2003, at the first Flip— an event that sprouted from her very own beautiful silver-haired head.

Liz Calder looks like Judi Dench, the actor who plays "M", James Bond's handler at MI6, the British secret service. The usual party jokers used to call her "Luiz Caldas", after the popular musician, though not to her face, of course. For many years, she had a small but very pleasant house further down the coast, accessible only by boat. Back in 2003, Lady Calder invited Flip's guests, Brazilian and foreign, to a feijoada party, and I went along as Marta's husband, since she published some of the local talent. On the schooner that took the literary troupe over I met the nonagenarian Eric Hobsbawm. The only one of his works I had read was that magnificent book about the 20th century, the name of which escapes me now. On the way out, I didn't dare talk to him. But on the way back, encouraged by a considerable amount of cachaça and beer (as always) I accosted him with a question: How did you like the feijoada, Mr Hobsbawm? To which the old sage responded, with a smile: Very good! That was the extent of my conversation with one of the 20th century's greatest intellectuals, still alive and kicking in the 21st. I don't know whether history will record it.

William Kennedy, a very modest man with the air of a pensioned-off grandfather in a less-than-prosperous American family, read a Hemingway story in a nasal, John Wayne voice.

I enjoyed listening to his cowboy American English, even if I didn't understand much of the story itself.

The other readers were Israel's Abraham Yehoshua, who read a heavy-going piece of Faulkner, perhaps in homage to the U.S., to which Israel is umbilically connected; Iranian Azar Nafisi, who went into agitprop mode and read poems about the struggle for freedom in her country; Ms Lionel Shriver, now fully clad in black, wearing tight trousers and see-through blouse, scrubbing up well for a fifty-something year old woman with a man's name, and still showing off her well-formed heel; someone called Pauline Melville, an actress-turned-writer born in Guiana who may or may not live up to the tremendous surname. She read a fragment out of "Bartleby, The Scrivener", by Herman Melville, to whom she might (or might not) be related.

Among the Brazilians, just me and Beatriz Bracher. The sweet and vaguely melancholic Bia Bracher, her hair ostensibly grey, is a banker's daughter but dresses like a left-wing militant of the Albanian line, which does not detract from her considerable charm. She is light-heartedness personified. She read a bone-dry passage out of Graciliano Ramos' *Angústia*, which would have changed the minds of anyone who thought literature was all about teatime pleasantries or wacky authors.

Directing the performance on stage was Liz Calder herself, who introduced the readers and then brought the proceedings to a close. After the usual applause, I could not resist going over to hug "Luiz Caldas", who looked at me with a benevolent and vaguely inquisitive air. I think James Bond's handler liked the unexpected intimacy with this illustrious...*who are you, again?*

The festival's grand finale was a cocktail party at the same Pousada da Marquesa that welcomed us upon arrival.

There I met the electric Ondjaki, a young Angolan writer with corn-rowed hair who now lives with a Brazilian woman in Rio. In between gulps of wine and snatches of high-flying conversation about writing and writers on both sides of the Atlantic, he offered to send details of his Portuguese publishers. I would not mind being published in the land of my maternal grandfather and my paternal great-great-grandparents. But it was boring to be talking about literature all the time, which is why I joined another writer –that was the only company to be found there—to take a few drags on a spliff behind some bushes in the garden, which inspired me to talk some more about –what else? Literature, obviously.

But before I forget –guess who was there, within ear-flicking distance? (Forget it, you'll never guess.) It was Crumb himself, in the flesh, with his white beard and his hat! *Oh yeah, man!* He, his wife Aline, and Gilbert Shelton with his wife Lora. The four of them spent a long time by a corner, talking quietly among themselves –to be honest, they were hardly talking—and drinking beer. Crumb sat on a stool in an almost foetal position, bent over and hugging his own knees, as I imagine the shiest of American teenagers would do if he found himself surrounded by strangers in a faraway country.

I instantly remembered the opening scene in the Terry Zwigoff documentary about Crumb, which I saw at the São Paulo Film Festival a long time ago. The film was simply called *Crumb*, and the scene showed him in exactly the same foetal position listening to a 78 rpm blues record, the needle scratching and squeaking over the vinyl. Success, I said to myself. Let anyone ask me now if I'd seen Crumb at Flip. —Sure!—I'd reply, quite full of myself, and dusting off my old school English. —Keep on trucking, baby!

The Authors

Beatriz Bracher was born in São Paulo in 1961. She began her literary career as editor of the magazine *34 Letras*, and as co-founder of publisher Editora 34. Her credits as a screenwriter include "Crónicamente inviável" (1994) and "Os inquilinos" (2009), co-written with Sergio Bianchi, and the script for Karim Aïnouz's "O abismo prateado" (2011). She published her debut novel, *Azul e dura*, in 2002. Her short story collection, *Meu amor* (2009), won the Clarice Lispector Prize, awarded by Brazil's National Library Foundation.

Born in Rio de Janeiro and now living in São Paulo, **Bernardo Carvalho** (1960) was a joint winner of the Portugal Telecom Brazilian Literature Prize for his novel *Nine Nights* (2002), and won both the Jabuti and the São Paulo Art Critics awards for *Mongolia* (2003). He has translated into Portuguese works by George Perec, Ian McEwan, Peter Carey and Oliver Sacks. His latest novel is *O filho da mãe* (2009).

Author, university lecturer and advertising copywriter **João Anzanello Carrascoza** (1962) was born in the town of Cravinhos, in the interior of the state of São Paulo. He wrote his earliest works for children, but it was through collections such as *O Vaso Azul* (1998), *Duas Tardes* (2002), *Dias Raros* (2004) or the more recent *Espinhos e Alfinetes* (2010) that he gained wide recognition as one of the finest Brazilian authors of short fiction.

Andréa del Fuego (born Andrea Fátima dos Santos, in São Paulo, 1975), began her writing career offering sex advice in a magazine column; she took her pen name from a burlesque dancer of the 1950s. Widely anthologised in volumes of short stories and flash fiction, she won the 2011 José Saramago Literary Prize for her first full-length novel, *Os Malaquías*, set in rural Minas Gerais. She contributes regularly to the television books programme, *Entrelinhas*.

Reginaldo Ferreira da Silva, known as **Ferréz**, was born in 1975 in the Capão Redondo district, in the southern periphery of São Paulo. He was already well known as a rapper, poet and cultural activist when he published his first novel, *Capão Pecado* (2000), inspired by daily life in his community. *Manual prático do ódio* (2005) continued his fictional exploration of the dilemmas faced by marginalised individuals for whom crime and violence are a means of survival.

Marcelino Freire (1967) was born in the town of Sertânia, in the interior of the state of Pernambuco, but began his writing career after moving to the state capital of Recife, where he joined the literary workshop run by novelist Raimundo Carrero. He is best known for his short stories, and for his work as publisher and literary promoter. His collection *Contos negreiros* (2005) earned him the Jabuti Prize in the short story category.

Milton Hatoum (1952) was born in Manaus, capital of the state of Amazonas, to parents of Lebanese origin. He went to school in Brasilia, studied architecture in São Paulo, and gained a postgraduate degree in comparative literature from Paris-Sorbonne University. He has published four novels – two of which (*Tale of a Certain Orient*, 1990, and *Ashes of the Amazon*, 2005) won Brazil's Jabuti Prize for Best Novel. His latest novel is *Orphans of Eldorado* (2008). He has translated into Portuguese works by Gustave Flaubert, Marcel Schwob and Edward Said.

Tatiana Salem Levy (1979) was born in Lisbon, where her parents had fled to escape Brazil's military dictatorship. She has published two novels: the largely autobiographical *The Key of Smyrna* (2008), winner of the São Paulo Literature Prize for best Brazilian debut novel, and *Dois Rios* (2011). She grew up and lives in Rio de Janeiro, is a translator of French fiction and non-fiction, and in 2012 was selected as one of *Granta* magazine's "Best of Young Brazilian Novelists".

Adriana Lisboa (Rio de Janeiro, 1970) won the José Saramago Literary Prize for her second novel, *Symphony in White* (2003). Her following works, *Um beijo de colombina* (2003) and *Rakushisha* (2008), were shortlisted for the Jabuti Prize. *Crow-Blue*, her latest novel, will be published in the United Kingdom in the autumn of 2013. She has translated works by Cormac McCarthy, Marilynne Robinson and Jonathan Safran Foer, among others. A trained musician and experienced singer, she has spent time in France and Japan, as is now living in the United States.

Reinaldo Moraes (São Paulo, 1950) gave up a career in economics and went on to become a cult author after the publication of his novels *Tanto Faz* (1981) and *Abacaxi* (1985). He has written screenplays for television, and between 2006 and 2011 hosted a regular radio show. His latest book is

Pornopopéia (2009). Among his translations into Portuguese are works by Thomas Pynchon, William Burroughs and Edmund White.

André Sant'Anna (Belo Horizonte, Minas Gerais, 1964) played bass in a rock band, composed music and worked in advertising before turning to literature. His first novel, *Amor* (1998), was followed by *Sexo* (1999) and *O Paraíso É Bem Bacana* (2006). His latest collection of short stories is *Inverdades* (2009).

Born in Lages, in the southern state of Santa Catarina, **Cristovão Tezza** (1952) moved at an early age to the city of Curitiba, in Paraná – the setting for most of his fiction. He is the author of more than a dozen novels, most notably *The Eternal Son* (2007), which won many of Brazil's most prestigious literary prizes (including the Jabuti Prize for Best Novel) and was later shortlisted for the IMPAC-Dublin Literary Award. His latest novel is *Um erro emocional* (2010). In 2011 he launched *Beatriz*, a new short story collection.

About the editor and translator:
Ángel Gurría-Quintana (1974) was born in Leeds, grew up in Mexico City, and now lives in Cambridge. A historian, journalist and translator of Spanish and Portuguese, he has written for the *Financial Times* since 2003, focusing on literature in translation. His work has also appeared in *The Observer, The Guardian, The Economist, Newsweek* and *The Paris Review*. He was one of the judges for Harvill Secker's 2013 Young Translators Prize.

First published in 2013 by Full Circle Editions

Introduction and translation copyright © Ángel Gurría-Quintana 2013
Original texts copyright © the individual authors 2013
Images copyright © Jeff Fisher 2013
The moral right of the authors and artist has been asserted.

The Language of the Future by Bernardo Carvalho, *Suli* by Beatriz Bracher, *The Cut* by Cristovão Tezza and *Flipping at Flip* by Reinaldo Moraes previously appeared in the anthology *Ten/Dez*, edited by Flávio Moura, published in Brazil in 2012 by Casa Azul.

Design and layout copyright © Full Circle Editions 2013
Parham House Barn, Brick Lane, Framlingham, Suffolk IP13 9LQ
www.fullcircle–editions.co.uk

A CIP record for this book is available from the British Library.

Set in Chronicle Deck & Gill Sans
Printed on 120gsm Amber Graphic FCS Mix Credit SGS-COC-004497 - carbon balanced

Book design: Jonathan Christie

Printed and bound in Suffolk by Healeys Print Group, Ipswich

ISBN 978-0-9571528-4-7

Note on the typeface:
Chronicle Deck forms part of Hoefler & Frere-Jones' Chronicle Display suite of fonts. Created in 2002, it revisits the Transitional 'Scotch' subspecies of typefaces (a form originating at the end of the eighteenth century associated with Scottish typefounders Alexander Wilson and William Miller) and blends it with the various demands of modern media. 'Scotch' signature details, like the pipe-shaped tail on the capital R, became traps for ink and pulp on early high volume presses — a problem that plagued every lowercase letter in the dainty 'Scotch' italic. Faces such as Chronicle and Matthew Carter's Miller (1997) bring strength and utility back to this classic serif.

www.flipsidefestival.co.uk

MINISTÉRIO DA CULTURA
Fundação BIBLIOTECA NACIONAL

Obra publicada com o apoio do Ministério da Cultura do Brasil / Fundação Biblioteca Nacional

This work has been published with the support of the Brazilian Ministry of Culture/National Library Foundation